Protecting the Poor

Protecting the Poor

Amanda Tero

Protecting the Poor

© 2019 by Amanda Tero

Published by Amanda Tero
Decatur, MS 39327

All Scripture references taken from the King James Version. Public domain.

This novel is a work of fiction. The characters in this story are fictitious. Any resemblance to persons living or dead is coincidental.

ISBN: 978-1-942931-30-0

Cover design by Amanda Tero
Images from
    www.pixabay.com
    www.shutterstock.com
Used by permission.

Formatted by Amanda Tero

To Reuben and Iris Barber

*You have become my third set of grandparents.
I cannot with words express how much your
lives have impacted mine with your love for
God, the church, and your family. I know that
you love me like one of your own, and I cherish
all of the memories I've made with you.
Thank you, especially, for supporting me
in my writing and always asking when the
next book is coming out.*

Character List

Lord Feroci – *previously Sheriff Feroci, of Abtshire*
Barat – *Lord Feroci's magnate*
Philaon – *Abtshire's stable master*
Dumphey – *prior stable hand, now a page*
Noel – *Dumphey's brother, also a stable hand*
Zuzene – *Dumphey and Noel's grandmother*
Lia – *formerly in Abtshire, now with Lord and Lady Kiralyn, called Ellia*
Lord and Lady Kiralyn – *Lia's parents*
Belle – *the king's daughter*
King Jarin – *the king of the land*

Prologue

$\mathcal{L}$ord Feroci slammed the desk with his fists. "I didn't send you on a fool's errand, Barat." He clenched his teeth as he glared at the missive opened before him.

"Aye, sir. I cannot help that others are the fools."

Feroci gave way to his anger in a growl. Barat stood patiently, his arms crossed.

"We're losing time, Barat."

His magnate didn't respond.

"You're not doing enough." He raised his head to glare at his man. Barat stared him down. Nothing could faze this man, which was exactly why Feroci had him in his employ. But 'twas irksome at times. Feroci blew out his pent-up air and fell back into his chair. "What do you suggest?" Barat was the only man in Abtshire from whom he would even consider suggestions. The man had proven his loyalty on the battlefield, taking more than one scar for Feroci. Feroci had returned the favor as many times. They were in this together.

Barat finally stepped forward, but he didn't sit in the seat across Feroci. Instead, he took the missive from Feroci's desk and held it at two corners. "I say we do this…" He pulled at the paper and it ripped—something weak giving way to a greater force that commanded it. That sight alone gave Feroci strength and he nodded in satisfaction.

"Aye. Something made from pulp cannot stand against an iron fist. They will give way."

"Call another meeting." Barat layered the two pieces of paper and held them over one of the candles that shed light in the dim room. A small strand of smoke wove upward before the paper burst into flame. Extra light illuminated the room then dimmed when Barat tossed it onto the tray. The paper turned to gray ash. "We know their weaknesses as well as their strengths. Use their weaknesses against them. Convince them that there is no other choice."

Feroci leaned forward and grabbed the quill he had dropped when Barat had entered. He ran his fingers across its smoothness before taking a clean paper. "Well put." He dipped the quill in ink. "Matheny … 'tis a vast city, but given the right promise, the townspeople will rebel and overthrow Lord Nedry." He wrote a few lines, shaping the concept that Barat had supplied. "Haar is closer to the king, so that could pose problems."

"Then wait on Haar. We've three cities between our province and them."

Feroci didn't look up from his writing. "Lord Alexandre is on my side. If he works with me, mayhap we can claim the help of Belmis, Metz, and Kiralyn." He paused at the last name. The anger that had dissipated boiled under the surface once more.

"You can't earn Kiralyn's—"

"Curse you, man!" Feroci threw his quill at Barat. He didn't flinch. "We'll have to overthrow Lord Kiralyn and sever any 'blood ties' to the king. I *will* obtain the throne." He stood and his chair crashed backward. Obtaining Lord Trent's domain from the king had been an easy task. The unfortunate lord had conveniently died in battle with no other witness besides Barat. The king had promoted Feroci from sheriff to lord, giving him reign over Abtshire, Fordyce, and Keller. Controlling the latter two was nothing—they were mere hamlets compared to the likes of Matheny. Feroci had the talent and ability for so much more.

He had to gain control before Yzebel gave birth to their child—his heir. It must be his heir. He had no use for a lass. But a son—a son he could shape and mold, without the meddling of others, to follow in his footsteps … aye, that son would establish their family as royalty forever.

The land was now under the leadership of a man who had gone mad since his daughter's return. Why had he named Princess Belle as heiress of the kingdom? She had left her father and had been raised by Lord and Lady Kiralyn. Feroci knew the details concerning the king's daughter better than anyone else in the province—he was one of the only men the king didn't refuse to see after the death of his wife. In the king's dark hours of grief, he had made substantial promises to Feroci for his help. Promises that had blown away much like the ash of the letter Barat had burned. 'Twas why Feroci had only just recently obtained lordship over Abtshire.

Feroci had written. Barat had spoken. Nothing would sway the king's mind. He was going against all tradition of the land by naming a woman as heir, making her the ruler of the kingdom, should he pass before she married.

"I can't marry the lass myself, and I haven't a son to do so. I will make the king pay," Feroci hissed. He walked to the window and pulled back the drapes that blocked the creeping fingers of dawn. A lad stood below, staring up at him. Recognition slammed Feroci when his eyes locked onto the lad. He was more of a threat to Feroci than he would ever know.

"Barat."

The man joined him.

"How much did he hear?"

The lad's gaze shifted to something in the distance. He turned and walked toward the barracks—the place he should have already been at this time of morning.

Barat's dark eyes followed the lad's movement. "You can finally make your move against him. He's as dangerous to you as Lord Kiralyn."

Finally. Feroci liked the sound of that word. "He's more dangerous." He had waited too long already. "Take care of him."

The silence between them sealed the promise.

"But don't make it a matter of suspicion." Feroci let the drapes fall. "I don't want to raise questions."

Chapter One

One Week Later

*D*umphey removed the last of the rye bread from his pouch. He had but a few minutes before training would begin at the barracks. He knocked on the door of Widow Anith. As soon as he heard footsteps approaching, he laid the bread in a cloth at the doorstep and hurried away. He watched from the shadows as the door opened and a young lass bent down to examine the bread. 'Twas the same lass who always came to the door, no more than four years of age. As always, she took the bread then looked around—as if making sure a soldier wouldn't steal it from her—before rushing back inside and shutting the door.

Another lass would not go hungry tonight. Warmth spread through Dumphey as he set off toward the barracks. Eight paces away, he stopped. Unease prickled the back of his neck. 'Twasn't the first time he felt like he was being followed this week. He spun around as a sword swiped toward him. He leapt backward. Pain sliced through his left arm. He fell to the ground and clutched his arm. Sticky blood pulsed under his grip.

They were supposed to train with wooden weapons. Not swords and armor. And definitely not a fully-armored soldier against unarmed page. Unless...

The knight lunged for him. Dumphey rolled, thwarting the attack.

This wasn't training.

He scrambled to his feet before the knight advanced again. He glanced around for something—anything—to use as a defense.

Nothing.

He stepped back. He was swifter on his feet than the armor-encumbered knight—but only if he could take his flight when the knight wasn't expecting it. Curse those wretched helmets with visors! He couldn't read the knight's intentions with metal shielding his eyes. He didn't even know who he was up against. Or why.

Surely the soldiers hadn't been spying on his actions around Abtshire and reported them to the lord. He had been cautious—hadn't he? Maybe not cautious enough. Dumphey sent up a silent prayer that God would protect the families he regularly visited.

They continued in a stalemate, circling each other. Dumphey kept his eye on the maille-covered arm that held the sword. The maille moved slightly. Dumphey ducked and the blade sliced over his head. Before the knight could make his next move, Dumphey turned and ran. His back was exposed, making him vulnerable, but run or stay, he faced death. He darted between cottages, slipping on trash that littered his way.

The nigh-completed walls of the barracks loomed before him. Just beyond it stood the stables. Dumphey risked a glance behind him. He had lost the knight, at least for the moment. He wove through another cluster of cottages until he reached the side of the stables away from the barracks. He slid through the open doors and slipped into the shadows before Philaon or Noel noticed him. Sweat soaked his tunic. Invisible spiders crawled up his legs after his sudden race. He closed his eyes and focused on silencing his gasping breaths as he pressed his hand to his wounded arm.

Here, with the comforting sounds of horses and the sweet smell of hay, was a safe haven. A place in which he had yearned to dwell this past year. With everything in him, he was grateful that Noel was still here instead of at the barracks. He had spent every day praying that Lord Feroci wouldn't force his younger brother into training. 'Twas bad enough, him being coerced to train and fight, when all he yearned for was peace in the land. But he wasn't given a choice. None of the lads were. They must fight for the lord or face the gallows. None of them could afford to pay Lord Feroci's conscription fee.

"Ah, there you are, my good lad." Barat's tone belied his congenial words.

Dumphey jerked, his fist forming. The lord's magnate. He held almost as much power as Feroci himself. How did he know to look here?

"Come with me." Barat placed a hand on Dumphey's shoulder and pushed him back toward the door—an order, not an invitation.

"I've done nothing wrong," Dumphey said as he stumbled outside with Barat. His mind raced. When had he not taken enough care? He always fulfilled his duties before escaping for just a few brief moments to distribute food. He was certain he avoided the soldiers on guard. *God, protect the others.* If his actions brought harm to others, he'd never be able to live with himself.

There was no sign of the knight in the streets. Dumphey wasn't sure if he should be relieved, now that he was under Barat's control. He stood straight, ignoring the throb of pain in his arm every time his heart beat.

"Nay, you have done nothing wrong. Yet."

Something was behind Barat's words. Something that snaked dread through Dumphey's body. He glanced at his wounded arm. The blood had ceased flowing. 'Twas only a scratch and would heal in time, but it had branded a scar in his heart. He would never let down his guard again. There was no place of safety in Abtshire anymore.

Barat stopped midway between the barracks and stables. "You have done well in your training, for all of the murmurings you gave."

Dumphey refused to respond. What lad would not do his best to survive training when his very life depended on it?

"Lord Feroci has a proposition for you." Barat lowered his voice. He looked out over the barracks, where dozens of peasant lads and lasses labored, lifting stones and spreading mortar. The barracks that had begun as soon as Feroci was given lordship would be completed within the fortnight.

Barat watched the workers for a moment, his dark eyes darting from the peasants to the soldiers who stood guard. Finally, he turned his gaze back to Dumphey. "The king will be sending men here. Today or tomorrow." His frown seared into Dumphey. "Philaon will be unavailable to answer the king's questions. You must be in his place. The lord will give you two pounds for this duty."

Two pounds? Dumphey shrugged away from Barat's grip.

"'Twould be more than enough for you to pay for your release from Lord Feroci's army. 'Tis what you want, is it not?"

Aye, but Dumphey wouldn't give Barat the pleasure of an agreement.

"Well, lad. The lord's request is simple. All is well at Abtshire. The peasants are happy. Lord Feroci is just in his dealings." Barat's dark eyes searched Dumphey's face as if threatening him with something. "He has only enough horses for the soldiers in his employ. You need say no more. If they ask after the barracks, tell them that the lord has not yet announced the purpose of his building, and the king's men must ask him directly."

Lies. All lies. Dumphey opened his mouth to speak, but Barat raised a hand.

"Remember, my good lad, if you refuse to do as the lord has requested, you will be sent to battle within the fortnight and the lad, Noel, will be sent to fill your place training in the barracks."

"Not Noel." The words slipped from his mouth before he could stop them.

A vile grin crept onto Barat's face. "The choice is yours." He folded his arms and leaned back, the smile unnatural on his lips. "What say you to the lord's offer? Speak as he requests or pay the consequences—aye, with your life." He nodded beyond Dumphey, and Dumphey followed his gaze to the knight. His sword was still drawn, decorated with a blotch of blood—Dumphey's blood. This was what the attack was about? Dumphey clenched his teeth.

"What choice, lad?"

There was no choice. Barat had intentionally placed a hedge about him.

"Speak now, lad, or…" Barat motioned to the knight, who took a step closer.

"I shall take the money." Dumphey hated himself, even as he spoke the words. But he couldn't place Noel's life in danger. 'Twas one of the only things he actually had a small portion of control over.

Barat's smile thinned as it spread broader across his face. He reached inside the pouch hanging from his side and withdrew a smaller pouch, which he held out to Dumphey. "Wise choice, my friend." He placed the bag in Dumphey's hand then held it with an iron fist. "You will be watched. One hesitation and you endanger both yours and the lad's lives."

Chapter Two

$\mathscr{D}$umphey watched as the horsemen left the stables and turned north to the king's highway. Tension had raced through the streets of Abtshire every moment they were here gleaning their report for the king. Money had been distributed to many hands from Barat's pouch with empty promises and bold threats. No one was brave enough to withstand the evil that oppressed them. There were only a dozen of the king's soldiers in Abtshire today compared to the scores of Lord Feroci's knights, soldiers, and squires decked in the red and yellow. Even if the king's men were on the side of the villagers, the lord had the greater force at play today.

Night would come soon. Dumphey left the stables. He would waste no time in settling matters with the lord. The pouch was well-hidden beneath the folds of his garment, but that wasn't safe enough. Nothing in Abtshire was safe.

He looked around him as he slowed his pace. Though a lad with a purpose, he didn't need to appear as such to the passersby and raise suspicion.

Someone moaned nearby and Dumphey stopped. 'Twas a wee lass, with flaxen curls hugging thin cheeks. He knew the cry well—'twas that of hunger. His hand rested on his pouch for a brief moment then moved as if he were brushing away traces of hay. He had coin enough only for his and Noel's freedom.

He glanced over his shoulder, the same feeling as yesterday haunting him. But no one seemed to be lurking in the shadows. 'Twas just his mind overreacting. On the morrow, as a free lad, he would see what he could do for the lass. She would still be there, still hungry. 'Twas the necessary step he must take in order to help more peasants.

Life in Abtshire had always been unfair, Feroci punishing the commoners at his own whims, caring nothing for the limitations of the aged or young. When he had hauled Zuzene away, Dumphey had been a small lad, Noel only a babe. There was nothing he could do for his grandmother. He had grown up, adjusted to life with Zuzene in the dungeon, never fully understanding why she was there or why Feroci never released her. She avoided his questions on the matter, so he submitted to the fact that he could do nothing about it. 'Twasn't what he liked, but he had grown complacent, calloused to the cries of men and women falling under Feroci's rule. Until Lia.

He had looked out for Lia more years than he could count. When Feroci dared to attempt hanging Lia on accusations rather than hard facts, Dumphey's eyes were opened.

Abtshire was a pit of injustice.

But his hands were tied. Just when he had started to form a plan to help feed those around him, he turned sixteen and was forced to enter the lord's barracks. 'Twas a hand-picked lot, those training at the barracks. Lord Feroci seemed to know everything about these lads. How, Dumphey wasn't sure. The lord didn't make it much of his business to confer with the peasants.

Now, though, freedom was on the horizon. His heart began to hope again even as guilt plagued his mind. He had accepted bribery for this freedom.

The sense that someone once again watched him silenced his thoughts. He turned. A man plowed into him, throwing him down. Pebbles dug into Dumphey as his opponent's weight pressed him to the ground. A dagger touched his throat. He twisted under his assailant's grip. The dagger pierced his flesh. He clenched his teeth and freed one hand. He gripped the man's hand. All movement froze.

"What do you want?" Dumphey gasped.

The man's eyes narrowed beneath the hood that shadowed his face, but he said nothing.

Dumphey hurled his body upward. His opponent's grip faltered. Dumphey clenched the dagger's hilt with both hands. His back scraped against the pebbles as he fought to free himself from the man's weight. The world darkened as the man's fist plunged into his face. When Dumphey's focus returned, the blade pointed toward his chest.

"What did you hear?" The man's voice was husky. Dumphey struggled to place it. Someone from his time at the stables? 'Twasn't one of his trainers. They would have killed him by now. "Speak, lad."

"Hear when?" He had the wrong lad. 'Twas the only rational explanation. Dumphey twisted his body as he forced the blade away. He plunged his elbow into the man's chest. A sharp inhale gave Dumphey courage to continue. With quick repetition, he jerked until the dagger was released from the man's grasp. Turning it, he plunged the blade into the man's shoulder then pulled it out. Though the man made no sound, his body relaxed for a brief moment. Dumphey pushed away before his captor could regain his strength.

He took four steps back, his heart pounding as the man writhed on the ground. His fingers froze around the dagger's handle as reality hit him. *God, let the man live.* Heaven forbid that he had taken the life of a man in the shadows of Abtshire. The man's chest rose and fell quickly. Relief spasmed through Dumphey. The man had but a shoulder wound. He would survive.

A scream penetrated the air. Dumphey spun toward the sound. Whichever lass had released it was hidden by the half dozen soldiers that ran toward him.

"Murderer!" The accusation hurled from one of the men advancing.

Dumphey sprinted away from the soldiers. A spear glanced the stones beside him, missing him by a handbreadth. A passageway between two cottages loomed before him. He looked back before taking the turn. A soldier stood over Dumphey's attacker, sword drawn and stained with blood. Dumphey tripped over a rut in the ground. He focused on his path. The soldier wasn't merely ascertaining the man's death—he was ensuring the man's death with a thrust of his own.

Dumphey darted between the cottages then pounded down the street. 'Twas a repeated nightmare from the day before—nay, 'twas worse. He would be branded a murderer and required to pay the price with his life. And he was being chased by soldiers—a group for which he was no match. Even as the thought crossed his mind, he fingered the belt at his waist. Given time to prepare, it made a fine sling—and pebbles were aplenty here. Yet he didn't have time.

He slipped into the shadows of the cottages and crouched behind a rotting crate. Noise rushed past him, mingling with the yellow and red of Feroci's men.

He couldn't return to the room he and Noel shared. If he was identified, 'twould be the first place the soldiers would look. The stables were not safe either. His heart beat a wordless prayer as his mind raced through the possibilities. Louvel's. The tailor would know the whereabouts of Patey. Surely in a time like this, Dumphey could count on the lad to help.

He checked behind him before nearing Commerce Row. Only two soldiers stood guard, seeming oblivious to the chase that was going on. Entering the shops from the back may be suspicious, but Dumphey didn't have time to formulate another plan. He pried the door open and stumbled into the small room. The bitter stench of black walnut hulls boiling for dye greeted him. He paused only long enough to hide the dagger in his belt before entering the main room.

Tailor Louvel stirred a simmering pot suspended above flames, his back to Dumphey. He didn't seem to notice the newcomer. Dumphey looked around the dimly lit room. His heart almost eased to normal pace when he saw Patey sitting in the corner. He waved his arms, not daring to risk Louvel sighting him.

Patey's eyes widened when he saw him, and he slid off the barrel and drew near.

"'Tis almost time for the watchman to come through. Why aren't ye..." Patey's voice faded as he squinted at Dumphey. "What scrape did ye find this time?"

"Not here," Dumphey said, nodding toward Louvel.

"The man can't hear. We're safe."

"Nay." Dumphey pressed himself against the wall, half-expecting the front door to fly open and soldiers to swarm through. As long as he was in Abtshire, there was no such thing as being safe. "Patey, I need to leave

Abtshire." As the words passed through his lips, his resolve strengthened. He hadn't believed his thoughts yesterday, but he was certain of it today. There could be no coincidence between the attacks. "They want me dead."

Chapter Three

*D*umphey stumbled behind Patey. His body screamed for him to go slower, to be considerate of the pain from two days' fighting against Lord Feroci's men. Dumphey had spilled his story to Patey in haste and was now rushing to keep up. Patey hadn't bothered to explain where they were going—it was just somewhere away from Abtshire.

"Patey—"

"Sh."

'Twas a sound laced with warning, but still, Dumphey couldn't heed it.

"Noel—"

Patey finally slowed. He whispered between gasps of air. "I'll care for the lad. Just come." He didn't give Dumphey a chance to respond before picking up his pace.

The night air fell silent around them. No breeze broke the stillness. It was as if all nature was holding its breath with Dumphey.

He plowed into Patey's back. Fire erupted from his wounded arm and he bit back a moan.

Patey gave a low, mournful whistle. Dumphey looked around him, even though his eyes couldn't penetrate the darkness of the night. Patey whistled again, then waited.

"This way," he said.

Dumphey followed without question, though dozens of them milled in his head. Noel would worry of his absence—how could he get word to him that he was safe? And what of the peasant children? The lass he saw today? Dumphey fingered the pouch that was still hidden beneath his tunic. He was out of Feroci's service now. If he had waited, would God have provided this way regardless? Dumphey tightened his fist around the coins. 'Twould be impossible to return without the lord's anger unleashed on him. Dumphey only prayed that Lord Feroci wouldn't take it out on Noel—or that Patey could return in time to take care of matters.

A glow of light peeked through the bushes—so faint, Dumphey wondered if he had actually seen anything. Patey plowed ahead without hesitation.

"Halt!"

Patey didn't stop, but Dumphey froze.

"'Tis Patey, ye dimwit." Patey walked toward a lad who brandished a bow and arrow. "Didna ye hear the call?"

A second lad joined the first. "What brings you here?"

Patey jerked his thumb back toward Dumphey. "My friend here needs your hospitality. The lord's men are after him for a crime he didna commit."

The lad snorted. "Another one, aye?" He turned his face toward Dumphey. "What are you called?"

"Dumphey."

"Your occupation?"

Dumphey hesitated. He wasn't exactly considered a soldier of the lord, even though he was in training. Yet he was no more a stable lad.

"Enough interrogation. I have to return afore I'm missed," Patey said. He stepped aside and pulled Dumphey forward. "This here's Betin." He nodded to the first lad who had greeted them. "And yonder is Dickie. There are other lads—all good lads. Betin'll introduce you." He raised a hand in farewell and disappeared into the night.

Betin stepped forward and offered a hand. "Welcome to our camp, Dumphey. As long as you're against Feroci, you've a place here."

"Thank you," Dumphey said. He followed Betin closer to the fire, embracing the warmth in the cool night's air.

"There are eight of us lads here." He nodded to the group by the fire. "Stefan and Arther." The first lad kept his brown head down, his face hidden. Arther was thin, his face serious as his dark eyes studied Dumphey.

"Simon, Cedric, Luther, William." Each lad nodded at Dumphey as their names were called. They were all limber lads, hair varying between the shades of wheat stalks and mud. Dumphey would place them around his age—mayhap Betin a year older, Dickie two years younger.

Dumphey studied the faces half-masked by darkness. 'Twould take him a full day to get each lad straight, if they even abode his presence that long. He could easily remember the two lads Patey introduced. A mischievous glint shone in Dickie's eyes as he measured Dumphey. Then, there was Betin—a tall red-head with freckles sprinkled on his face. He was the leader of this group, Dumphey assumed.

"What's your crime?" Dickie asked.

One of the lads around the fire shook his head, though a grin hinted on his features. "Mayhap we should ask why Patey figured he'd be a good addition to our group."

Betin shushed the two and poked a stick at the fire. "Neither of you have room to talk. I trust Patey's judgment."

Dickie laughed a short, sardonic laugh while the tall, somber lad—Stefan?—rose and left the group.

"Aye, we all trust Patey." Dickie winked at Dumphey. "He's the only one of us who can get away with the pranks he pulls in Abtshire. The grand lord has no idea who he entertains when he gets fittings for a new wardrobe. I keep waiting for the day we get news that Feroci has beheaded him."

"Dickie." The reproof from Betin didn't hold much seriousness.

Dickie threw up his hands. "Of all the scornful mockery in history, Betin. Patey has gone by with far more crimes than me—yet he remains unscathed, free to roam the countryside and do his mischief."

"Which is more than any of us can say. Curse Lord Feroci." The lad who spoke had his face drawn in a harsh frown.

"Cedric, speak not evil of the man," Betin said.

"Easy for you to say. Who have you left in Abtshire? A sister, aye? Who have I? Feroci took the lives of everyone I cared for—and would have had my skin too, were it not for the forest." Cedric's eyes flashed brighter than the fire into which he stared.

Betin didn't reply, but turned his back to Dumphey and rummaged through a pile. "Have you had dinner?"

"Nay." The pain from his injuries had masked hunger pangs, but now he felt them in full force.

"We haven't much, but I wager 'tis more than your portion in Abtshire." Betin turned and held out a chunk of bread. "Dickie's eaten all of the stew."

Dumphey took a bite out of the bread. Dickie snickered as he spoke to Betin, "Your portions make the lord's appear like generosity. Even *he* wouldn't blame me for scraping the pot."

"You should be shamed," Betin said, "to have a greater portion than a babe in Abtshire and make light of it."

"Ah, but we're not in Abtshire," Dickie retorted. "We are free men." He lay out on the ground, arms folded under his head. "All of nature is ours to do with as we please. We hunt the lord's food, you know." He turned toward Dumphey. "Snatch the pheasants right from under his nose at times, Arther and I do. Aye, Arther?"

The lad didn't give a response other than a half-grin. He still sat silently, studying Dumphey as he ate.

"Simon'll join us. At times, Luther. In one day, the four of us snared a dozen pheasants. That would cost— what think ye? A full gold crown? Nay, we got them free, and Feroci is none the wiser."

"Stop your boastings." Betin nudged Dickie with his foot as he settled back down. "If Dumphey is to be a part of our clan, he needs more than your empty-headed talk."

"Ha!" Dickie rose up on one elbow. "And who put you the leader of the group?"

"Let Betin talk," Arther said, tossing a chunk of dirt at the youngest lad. "He was leader before you came along, and you aren't going to be changing things by empty wheezing."

Dickie glared but shut his mouth.

Betin turned his full attention on Dumphey. "We move often, to not attract the attention of the lord's guard.

They rarely come out this far. And when they do, 'tis only one or two. Are you good with an arrow?"

Dumphey swallowed the dry crust he was chewing. "I've never had an opportunity to try. A sling is the closest thing I have for a weapon." Well, that and the dagger he had acquired today from the fight. He hadn't much experience with it, though. Even in all of the months training in Feroci's barracks, he wouldn't be trusted with a sword until they were out on the battlefield—something Dumphey was relieved to miss.

"We shall see what you can do, then. We never kill." A dangerous look passed over Betin's face as he stared at Dumphey then each of the lads seated around the fire, as if to remind them of this fact.

Dumphey's throat tightened and he choked on the dry bread. He didn't kill that man—nay, 'twas one of the sheriff's own men. Nonetheless, guilt tore at him. He took the tin of water that Arther passed to him and gulped.

"Our only goal is to survive without them killing us. When I give word to leave, we leave—quickly, quietly, and without a trace that we have been here." He motioned toward the darkness, where Stefan had disappeared. "We take turns standing guard. A sharp eye is needed. You must learn the calls." He cupped his hands and gave a low, mournful whistle. "This is the signal Patey used—we use it to communicate our location." A quick, high-pitched call followed. "Danger." Then, he removed a thin, wooden piece from the pouch at his side. "Stefan will make you a whistle and teach you the other calls. These are our codes for survival."

Dumphey nodded. Survive. He was an outlaw now. He had no other choice but to follow the rules here.

"Choose you a bed." A grin teased Betin's mouth as he gestured to the thick bed of leaves surrounding them. "We're quite generous in that area." Apparently finished with his speech, he set his bow and quiver beside him and lay down.

Dumphey walked several paces away from the fire and stretched out, facing the lads who were closer to the warmth. Dickie's chest rose and fell in the steady rhythm of sleep. Arther's body was as motionless as Betin's. The other lads were either asleep or close to it. Dumphey turned his face toward the heavens, staring at the plethora of stars winking at him through the treetops. This was it, then. His first eve as a criminal. He closed his eyes only to see the limp body of the man whose dagger he now possessed. He hadn't killed him. The wound in his shoulder may have maimed him, but there was still life in the stranger's body. But what was his word against a soldier's when it came to Lord Feroci? Aye, leaving Abtshire before he was unjustly charged with murder was the wise thing to do.

What did this mean for Noel? Uncertainty gripped him, driving all thoughts of sleep away. Barat knew him well. He knew Noel. He would know that Dumphey had left the barracks without paying his fees. Would he try to get them from Noel? Dumphey had to get the coins to his brother, and soon. 'Twould ensure the lad a way to escape. Patey would know how to get this task done and make certain Noel's safety.

Something lingered at the edge of Dumphey's mind. The man who had attacked him ... there had to be a reason behind it. He was known on the streets of Abtshire as a lad who did well by the people.

What did you hear?

The man's raspy words echoed in his mind. Dumphey's skin crawled with invisible terror. 'Twasn't about the money. 'Twas about something else. Was it connected to his good will toward the peasants? If only Dumphey knew.

Chapter Four

Noel lay on his back and stared at the darkness around him. Hours had passed since he had heard the watchman make his circuit, calling all townspeople to return to their cottages. 'Twas the second evening since he had seen Dumphey in the stables. The same day that Dumphey had been accused of murder. Rumor had spread that Dumphey was to be hanged—openly, for all to see the penalty of his misdeed. Yet that hadn't happened.

Father, I fear for my brother. Keep him from darkness and the powers of this world. Protect him from the soldiers tonight. 'Twas the same prayer he had prayed the last even, but he couldn't think of another prayer. Not until he knew something. But there was no one he dared ask about Dumphey.

He turned to his back and stared up at the darkness. He and Dumphey had lived in this room since before Mother passed—and she was a distant memory. Yet Noel could remember her stroking his head at nighttime when he was afraid in this small, dark room above the cooper's shop. She had often placed her fingers under his chin and tilted his face up to look at hers, and together they would count up the blessings of this place.

"'Tis a roof over our head," Noel whispered, "Shelter from the wind, protection from the snow, provision from God, a place to—"

Soft thumps sounded on the stairs that led up to his door. Noel sat up and waited, scarcely taking a breath. If it wasn't Dumphey, would it be someone informing him that Dumphey was caught? What if the morrow saw Dumphey on the gallows? Or worse, what if he found Dumphey beaten to death, no chance given for trial? Noel shut his eyes tightly and began praying.

Fresh air swept into the room then the door was closed with scarcely a sound. Noel's eyes flew open. The shuffle on the wooden planks was soft, yet 'twasn't Dumphey's shuffle.

He pulled himself into a ball and bit his lip to keep from crying aloud.

"Noel?" The voice scarcely broke the death-like silence.

Noel's words caught in his throat. He couldn't speak. Couldn't breathe. Who was this?

The stranger came closer. All strength left Noel's body. Were something to happen to him, who would inform Dumphey?

"Noel, 'tis Patey. A friend of Dumphey's."

The mention of his brother sent renewed strength through Noel and he released the air he had been holding.

"Dumphey is safe."

Tears formed in Noel's eyes. He wiped them away. A lad of his age didn't cry, no matter what happened. Or so Dumphey had told him so many years ago when he was frightened because of nighttime's darkness. At times, Noel felt that Dumphey saw him the same way as he had when younger—a small child to be soothed and sheltered. Sometimes Noel looked at himself the same way. Dumphey was so much bigger and bolder. He would never fear darkness, much less have been afraid when a stranger entered. He would have taken action and not let the stranger say the first word. And if Noel was the one missing, Dumphey would do everything in his power to ensure his brother was safe. He wouldn't have waited until someone came and set his fears at ease.

But what could Noel—a lad of twelve, barely entering manhood—do?

"Where—where is he?" He finally found the words to ask.

Patey blew out a breath. "Just be assured he is safe and will stay safe."

He was holding something back—a big something. But Noel was too scared to ask what.

"He didn't really kill anyone, did he?" Noel shouldn't have to ask. But there had been times when he'd see a look cross over Dumphey's face. How he wished he could read the thoughts behind those looks. Not knowing scared him.

"Nay," Patey said, his voice firm and sure in the darkness. "Dumphey didna kill a soul. 'Twas Lord Feroci's own men, to put a target on Dumphey's back."

"But … why?" It didn't make sense. Dumphey had been nothing but faithful as a stable lad, and more recently, as a page in training.

Patey released a growl loud enough to make Noel jump and wish he would be quieter during the night hours. "I'm going to discover that." His voice softened. "For now, Dumphey asked ye to oversee caring for the peasants."

Noel's stomach rolled and he rubbed his hands over his arms to stop the sudden tingling. He had helped Dumphey collect food for the poorest—but never had Dumphey let him come along to distribute the goods. 'Twas too dangerous, he had said. What had changed his mind?

"What if I haven't time to properly do as much as Dumphey? I just gathered the food."

"Leave the food gathering to me," Patey said. "Ye may use that time to distribute. Dumphey said ye know the families."

Aye, Noel had helped Dumphey find the seven families to help—one for each day of the week. 'Twas so little they did, but now, Noel was determined that Dumphey's absence wouldn't make that little even less.

Silence stretched between them for a moment, then Patey ground out, "'Tis time someone shows Feroci his ways are wrong." His voice was dangerously determined. "The man feasts in his castle with wine and food enough to feed the entirety of Abtshire. I've beheld it, Noel. Every time I enter the castle to help Louvel fit Feroci and his family for new clothes. 'Tis a disgust for any province under the name of our good king. Feroci knows the trials of his peasants and he refuses to do a thing. If ye only saw it, Noel. It makes even a good man wish to kill the lord and place a just ruler in his stead."

Noel's jaw dropped open. "But…"

"But what?" Patey snapped the question out, and Noel wished it was Dumphey who was here talking to him. Not a stranger on Dumphey's behalf. Dumphey understood him. Patey didn't.

Noel swallowed. The story of David with Abigail's husband flashed before his mind. God had killed Nabal in His own time. Could not He do the same for someone like Lord Feroci? If, indeed, the lord was as much at fault as Patey suspected.

"I know ye and Dumphey have done a good work in Abtshire, distributing food for the hungry. But 'tis time. We must do more than merely distribute food."

"We?" Surely Patey wasn't expecting Noel to join hands with him in a rebellion.

"Aye. Betin's men, Dumphey, ye, me."

Patey shouldn't be counting on him. Dumphey was bold enough to run away from the lord and escape—he had training from the lord's barracks. But if Noel tried, he knew that he'd end up in the stocks—or worse, hanging. Just the thought of a thick cord touching his neck sent shudders of fear through his whole body.

"We must take action. Payback for cruelty." Patey spoke intensely, his tone getting short.

The air fell stiff and silent between them, pressing into Noel. He didn't dare speak for fear of what Patey may say next.

Was this what Dumphey thought too? *Oh, Father, I am worried for Dumphey.*

He couldn't join in a rebellion against the lord—even if the lord was as wicked as Patey supposed.

"Could you take me to Dumphey?" Noel whispered. Dumphey usually knew what he was talking about. He was wise for his age and had proved himself over and over. But to blatantly go against the lord? Dumphey knew the verses Zuzene quoted about honoring those in authority and praying for them. Would Dumphey agree with this lad Patey or put him in his place?

"Nay." The coarse fabric of Patey's tunic rustled in the darkness. "'Tis best if ye didna know where he is, lest the lord asks ye." His voice grew more distant. "Do not disclose our conversation with anyone. Have I your word?"

"Aye." Noel was too scared to trust anyone now. Even Zuzene couldn't be told of this—for there was usually a soldier nearby who could hear their words.

"Rest well."

A soft *thud* notified Noel of the door closing, then all was silent. He was alone again. Alone, and harboring a secret he hadn't asked for. One that he mustn't dare let slip for anything.

He lay down on the straw that made up his bed. How he wished Dumphey were here tonight. How he wished all was well in Abtshire. How he wished for a semblance of peace in his life. Yet instead, his heart was overloaded. He squeezed his eyes shut to pray. If desires could change hearts, then he had enough to make every wrong in the world right.

Chapter Five

'Twas daybreak, yet the lads had been busy since the stars were still clearly visible. Three days, and they had moved camp three times. They seemed to follow the same routine. Betin sent three lads out scouting, two lads hunting, and the rest packed and moved camp during the early morning hours.

Only when they finished setting up their new camp did Dumphey dare to strike up a conversation with one of the lads—a lad whose arms were almost as long as his body. 'Twas either Simon or Cedric. He couldn't tell the lads apart yet, given how little they were actually in the same vicinity.

"Is this all you do?"

The lad snapped a stick in two and laid it on the pile he had begun. He looked at Dumphey, his brows raised in question.

"Run from one place to another, not really knowing whether or not Lord Feroci is after you."

"Oh, he's after us." Cedric—or Simon—said. "He's after *you* for certain." He nodded, his lips drawn into a fierce frown. "Simon has seen him." So this lad must be Cedric. "So has Stefan. 'Tis why we keep moving." He struck two rocks together, directing the spark toward the dry sticks. He turned his glare from the sticks and settled it on Dumphey, his brows low. "Until *you* came, we could stay in one place for days."

"That's enough," Betin interrupted. His arms were loaded with thick sticks as he walked closer. "We watch each others' backs here. 'Tis what we do. If we can't stay together, there is no doubt but that Abtshire will lose hope."

Cedric snorted. "What hope is there left in Abtshire? I have no plans for returning. If you could bear to tear yourself away from your beloved sister," sarcasm hung on every word, "we would be escaping o'er the mountains right now."

A red flush stole over Betin's face as he threw the wood down. His jaw ticked and he clenched his fists, but he didn't look at Cedric.

"I know that we'd be safe on the other side. Feroci's men can't stop us from leaving his province, no matter how much he desires it. He may have control over Abtshire. But here?" Cedric waved toward the trees that surrounded them. "Here, 'tis our territory." He glared at

Dumphey, the pointed look sending ice through Dumphey's veins. "First it was Stefan. Then Dickie. Now Dumphey. We'll have half the village here afore long, if you don't see the wisdom in my plans."

"Leave, then." Betin's voice was low and strained, unlike Dumphey had heard him thus far.

Cedric stared at Betin, his eyes narrowing. "Nay, you don't mean it."

"Aye," Betin said. "If you wish to leave, I'm not holding you back." He raised his arms and opened his hands, as if signaling Cedric's release. But his hands were trembling.

"I take half the resources," Cedric said.

A vein in Betin's neck became visible. Dumphey took a step back, expecting any moment to erupt in fisticuffs.

Cedric placed another stick on the fire that was now kindling—they kept the fire small, fed with dry sticks to avoid excess smoke. He stood, wiped his hands, and walked to the other end of camp, where two other lads were gathered.

Dumphey watched as Betin spun around and marched away to the woods. 'Twas his fault, this fight they had. He shouldn't have gone to Patey. Surely there was another way out of his scrape. Yet, even as the thought crossed his mind, he knew 'twasn't possible. Mayhap if he had a way to reach Kiralyn Castle, to find Lord Kiralyn and Lia...

He tamped down the thought. He hadn't heard a word from Lia since she had found her father and left Abtshire.

'Twas for the better, Dumphey was sure. Lord Kiralyn was respectable enough. And rich. He could care for Lia better than anyone in the mire of Abtshire could even think of.

He raced after Betin. He didn't know what words to say, but surely he could do something to make amends. Something to keep the group together. He stopped when he saw Betin again. The lad had his bow drawn. A second later, there was a light *whiz* then thud as the arrow hit its target. Without waiting, Betin pulled another arrow and released it. Then another and another. Only when Betin's quiver was empty did he stop and move forward to retrieve them. When he turned to walk back, his eyes lit on Dumphey and he paused.

"What do you need?"

Dumphey shook his head. "Nothing." He took a step closer. The fire was gone from Betin's eyes. In its place was a look Dumphey had seen and known all too well— that of a young lad who held more responsibility than he could shoulder.

"Well," Dumphey said. "I came to ask your forgiveness."

Betin turned the bow in his hand. "Methinks you're not the one in need of apologizing."

"But, had I not come—"

Betin held up a hand to stop the words. "Cedric is looking for any excuse to do what he wants. What he chooses is his alone to bear. 'Tisn't your doing. You're here to stay, Dumphey." His green eyes shone in sincerity before he looked away, off toward the direction of camp. "This time, if I'm not mistaken, Cedric will leave in earnest." He shook his head.

"Would it not be safer elsewhere?"

"Mayhap." Betin slowly returned the arrows to the quiver on his side. "But I cannot leave Lydda in Abtshire, and I cannot take her with me. She's a strong lass in spirit, but not in health. What of you?" He turned his focus from the arrows to Dumphey. "Cedric will not turn you down if you ask to go with him."

Dumphey shook his head. 'Twasn't even a choice in his eyes. "I have my own family in Abtshire with which to be concerned."

Chapter Six

Noel slipped bread to the little lad. Hidden between the slices was a thin slab of cheese, somehow obtained by Patey. There was no response besides the lad's eyes widening. He didn't dare to meet Noel's gaze, and it smote Noel's heart. Dumphey had been right when he had said that times were rapidly changing in Abtshire.

Dumphey. His disappearance was but proof of those changes.

He continued down the street, wishing he could catch sight of his brother. Just as much as he wished he could drown out the cries of the hungry babes. Nay—he wished for more than that. He wished he could silence them by fulfilling their every need. But he was just a lad himself. It had been more days than Noel could count since he and Dumphey had begun seeing to the needs of the poorest around them. Whether it was from what little they could spare or from others who knew of this mission, they always had something to hand out. Since Lord Feroci had sent Dumphey to the barracks, they had ceased working together, but they had found a way to still faithfully meet the needs of others.

But for every peasant they fed, there were ten and twenty more, their sallow faces begging Noel to offer more. He could never do enough. There was always a gaping void. And no matter how often Zuzene reminded him that it was God alone Who could fill every void and He didn't hold Noel accountable for the wicked acts of others, Noel still wished he could do more.

Was it true, then, what Patey said? Was it indeed time to do more than just suffice the needs of those around him? Was it time to take action?

With the last crumb gone, Noel returned to the stables. Daylight was just beginning to peek into the shadows, revealing the dust dancing around in the air. He flung open the doors, letting as much of the light into the dark interior as possible. He walked to the leather tack that the lord would expect cleaned this morn, but his mind drifted to the place in the back of the stables where he had hidden the coins Patey had given him the day before.

Patey had said they were Dumphey's coins, intended to free Dumphey from the lord's army—except now Dumphey didn't need it. And he wanted Noel to have it, lest Lord Feroci would conscript him as well.

Noel ran his rag over the straps of the harness. Were the coins acquired by unjust means? Not Dumphey. He wouldn't act in a way that wasn't wholly upright. Yet how did he suddenly come upon them? Surely he hadn't been saving them without giving to the poor. 'Twasn't like Dumphey.

Metal clanked against metal and Noel jumped to his feet. He grabbed a nearby pitchfork, backed into an empty stall, and held it to his pounding chest. The stall darkened as three figures stood before him, blocking out the cheer of the early morning's rays.

"Ah, what have we here?" Barat barked out the question then leered as he leaned forward. "My good lad, have you seen Dumphey?"

"M—my…" Noel's throat went dry and his mouth refused to form a word. This was what Patey had warned him would happen. He was at Barat's mercy.

"Aye!" The magnate jerked the pitchfork away from Noel and flung it across the stables. It clattered as it fell against the compacted clay in the center. "You two do everything together, even when you oughtn't. You know where he is. Tell us!"

"Nay, sir." Noel cowered, but his back was pinned against the wall of the stall and prevented him from going further. "I haven't seen him since he—several days ago." He hadn't seen Dumphey since the last moment when he and Barat had been talking, here at the stables. Even then, Dumphey hadn't spoken to him directly.

"Since he…?" Barat echoed Noel's words, a mocking grin on his face. He stepped forward, his hot breath burning on Noel's forehead. He enunciated each word slowly, "Where did he go?"

"I know not." Noel tried to stand still, but his knees weakened and he slid down an inch. *Oh, Father, protect me. Protect Dumphey.*

Barat clenched Noel's shoulders and brought him back up to his full height. "Oh, I doubt that. You will tell us, and you will tell us soon." He sneered down at Noel. "He's wanted for murder. Did you hear? He's a murderer."

Noel swallowed, but his throat was dry as the dust that packed the ground. Dumphey was no murderer. His eyes darted from Barat to the two men who were with him.

"I saw it meself." One of the soldiers stepped up beside Barat. "Killed a man. Stabbed him in the chest, he did."

Stabbed? But Dumphey hadn't a weapon. Nay, Noel chose to believe Patey. Chose to believe his brother's integrity.

"He stole from the man, too," the other soldier added. "A full sack of coins." He shook his head slowly.

Noel's stomach flipped inside him. Was that indeed where the coins had come from? And if so, then which account was truth? "H-how do you know 'twas…" He licked his dry lips, but even then, his brother's name faltered on his lips. "Dumphey?"

One side of Barat's lips lifted in a grin. He loosened his grip on Noel's shoulder then patted him. 'Twasn't the brotherly-love type of pat that Dumphey sometimes gave, nor the one of compassion often extended by Zuzene. Nay, this was an act of mockery. "One of your own people—Idonia—witnessed the scene. Aye, Dumphey is not the dutiful lad we once thought him to be." He jerked a dagger from his belt and held it in front of Noel's face. "We need to know his whereabouts."

"I—I haven't seen Dumphey."

"Then you will tell us when you do see him," Barat said, pressing the dagger's tip into the soft tissue of Noel's ear. "Or you shan't be able to hear what he tells you when he does return."

Noel tried to swallow, but his muscles didn't work. Nodding might pierce the blade of Barat's dagger into his flesh, so he croaked out, "Aye."

Barat stepped back and Noel's knees buckled, sending him to the stall floor in a heap.

"Let us not keep you from your tasks," Barat said. "Wouldn't wish to pull your job out from under you."

The men laughed and their footsteps pounded as they retreated in a flash of the lord's red and yellow. Tears rose in Noel's eyes as his body shuddered. He had to find Patey and send word to Dumphey—to warn him. Whatever plans it was that his brother had lined up, he must be cautious. Lord Feroci's men were already waiting for him. He sat up and drew his knees to his chest, willing his body to calm down. He was safe. God had protected him. He took a deep breath and released it. But for how long?

Chapter Seven

*D*umphey swung his sling around—once, twice, thrice. He released his index finger and watched the cobble speed through the trees, narrowly missing his target. He grimaced. Granted, the sapling was but three fingers' width. Were it a man, the cobble would have made its mark. But still, he wished to do better. No matter how many thousands of times he practiced, though, t'was nigh impossible to make perfect aim with the sling.

A low, mournful whistle blended with the breeze. Patey's whistle. He wrapped his sling around his waist and darted through the woods.

"Did you find him?"

"Aye." Patey shifted the sacks that he had on his back.

"And...? He took the money? Did he say anything of the barracks?"

"Nay." Patey kept walking forward.

"How is he?"

Patey looked sideways at Dumphey then lowered the sacks. "If ye're going for a chat, ye haul one of these."

Dumphey took half the burden and walked beside Patey.

"Noel wonders if 'tis true ye murdered a man and stole his money." Patey's own look was full of suspicion—though it was tinted with admiration.

The force of his statement hit Dumphey like a horse charging at him full speed. "Who told him of this?"

"He said Barat visited him—"

"Barat." Dumphey spat the word out. Never had he experienced such distaste for a man as he did now. Feroci may be evil, but Dumphey had few personal dealings with the man since he had become lord. He should have pieced it together sooner. Barat had created a neat little parcel— first with the bribery and then with the murder. The fool he was for falling prey to this trap. 'Twas what he got for not seeking God, and now he'd have to pay the repercussions.

But why target Dumphey? He didn't like the man, but he never did anything against his commands. And there was no law against helping those in need from one's own resources—besides, Dumphey and Noel were careful to help others only on their time, not the lord's. And they did it without fanfare.

"I'll keep an eye on Noel for ye," Patey said.

Concern overrode any appreciation Dumphey may have felt. "He is in danger?" At least, more danger than just being a peasant of Abtshire.

Patey shifted his sack, his eyes scanning their new camp. "What of Cedric and his lads?"

Dumphey gritted his teeth. He wasn't ready for the subject to change from one unpleasant topic to yet another. "They left. We haven't seen them since." He had been worried about the ruckus they had raised, but the departure was silent—Cedric took with him Simon, Luther, and William, leaving Betin, Arther, Dickie, Stefan, and Dumphey.

"Good riddance," Patey growled as he handed his sack over to Arther. "Cedric didna like me much anyway."

Dumphey didn't reply. He figured Cedric didn't like anyone but himself.

"Ah, Patey, our good man." Arther slapped him on the back. "What have you brought this time?" He took the sack from Dumphey and began rummaging through its contents. "From the lord's larder, aye?" A wide grin stretched on his face.

Disbelief flickered through Dumphey. "You steal from the lord?" Unease flickered through him at the accusation. He had lied for Feroci. Was there any difference? Zuzene quoted Scriptures about offending in one point of the law, yet being guilty of breaking them all.

Patey shrugged. "What I do is none of your concern. Ye have more food than just wild game. Be grateful.

Though," he looked from Arther to Betin, "'Tis my usual fare and we've only half the lads to eat it."

"Then distribute it to the poor," Dumphey said, his voice gruff. *Hypocrite. White-washed hypocrite.*

"Already accomplished," Patey said as the others eyed Dumphey uncertainly.

The answer didn't rest well with Dumphey. He pushed away any thought of the bribe he had accepted to focus on this. Mayhap he was attempting to cast out Patey's mote while the beam was in his own eye, but Patey's life hadn't been threatened. He had simply stolen because he could. 'Twas wrong to steal, even for a good act.

Arther shook his head emphatically. "There are too many poor in Abtshire for us to see to all their needs."

"So we live in pleasure and satisfaction while they starve?" Dumphey asked.

Betin's hands slowed as they removed hunks of cheese and bread from the sacks. "I hadn't thought of it that way." He looked up at Dumphey. "Our families are cared for—Patey sees to that afore he brings us our food. But I remember hunger well. We feast out here."

"Food!"

Dickie charged into camp with a gleeful laugh. He snatched the bread from Betin's hand and tore off a bite. "Mmm ... fresh, too. From the bakery today, aye?"

Patey shrugged, but his smile gave away the answer.

"Surely there is some way we can spread this good fortune to others in Abtshire?" Dumphey couldn't release the idea. His conscience stung him when he considered from whence the food had come, but 'twas too late to undo that damage now. Were he the leader and could change things…

Dumphey pushed the thought aside. Betin was the leader, and he did well by it.

"What good fortune?" Dickie asked.

"Sharing our food with Abtshire," Arther said.

"Ha!" Dickie pinched a piece of bread off with his fingers this time. He held it up to Dumphey. "If we give each peasant a portion this size, aye, we'd have enough to share."

Dumphey folded his arms together and looked at Betin. So far, he was the only lad who showed any sign of reason. "I cannot abide the thought of babes starving to an early grave while we live healthy in the forest."

"And how would we go about helping them?" Betin asked.

"Patey may be sly," Arther said, "but we want to keep him in Abtshire. It benefits us all. So he can't do it."

"I'll do it." The soft voice came behind them.

Dumphey turned and beheld Stefan. He hadn't heard the lad speak but once or twice in the days he had been in the group.

"But you're in trouble—"

"Aye." Stefan took a step forward, determination resonating from his whole body. "Dumphey is right." He nodded toward Dumphey with a look of admiration.

Dumphey held Stefan's gaze for a few seconds. He hadn't attempted to earn the respect of the lads here, but he knew with that one look from Stefan that he had. The thought warmed him more than the fires that Betin erected each eve.

"If we're returning to Abtshire, let me go too," Dickie said.

The lad would get himself in trouble with his thirst for adventure. Dumphey suspected he cared more for the thrill of excitement than he did doing good for the poor.

"We'll let Dumphey make the decision," Betin said. "'Tis his idea."

Dumphey studied the faces of the lads before him. Betin and Stefan showed full support. Arther, indifference. Patey and Dickie, excitement. He shook his head slowly. "Is there a way we can provide for the poor without … thievery?" He had to call it what it was.

Betin looked down at the toe of his shoe and scuffed it in the dirt. By his thoughtful look, Dumphey knew he was considering. Patey shook his head, that half-smile on his face—almost as if he wanted to accept a challenge more difficult than stealing from the lord's larder.

"We provide them meat." Once more, it was quiet Stefan who spoke. He gestured toward the wood around them. "The lord may believe he owns everything here, but 'tis God Almighty's own land and the creatures He gave mankind to freely eat."

Dumphey nodded, his esteem of Stefan growing. He turned a questioning gaze to Betin.

Slowly, Betin looked at the lads around him. "All this time, we've complained of Feroci stealing from our families." He paused and his words sank in, giving Dumphey hope that the right choice would be made. "I stand behind Dumphey's decision. We shan't repay evil for evil, but will provide that which is honest in the sight of all men."

Betin placed a hand on Dumphey's shoulders, and the weight of the lad's respect settled on him like a cloak. He didn't want to fail this trust.

Chapter Eight

$\mathcal{D}$umphey sat by himself, watching as the lads dispersed the food and separated to attend their individual tasks until only he and Betin were left. Betin was on the far side of camp, a long piece of wood in his hand. 'Twasn't the first time Dumphey had noticed Betin set apart, his hands busy while he sent others to watch for soldiers or forage for food. Dumphey walked up to him. "What is that?"

Betin knelt down and opened the bag beside him, pulling out a dagger.

"Weapons?" Dumphey's heart sped up. The only weapons he had seen of this quality were those in Abtshire's barracks—and the dagger he wished he had never grabbed hold of.

"Tools." Betin continued digging and came out with a ball of twine.

Dumphey's eyebrows rose. "You didn't steal—"

"Nay! If Algor taught me one thing, 'twas to never take that which is not rightfully mine." He lowered his gaze and shrugged his shoulders, as if apologizing for what he had allowed his lads to do.

"Algor?" The name struck a chord in Dumphey's memory and he inhaled sharply. "The man who was hung for treason?"

Betin's green eyes flashed and he shook his head violently. "Algor was as loyal to the king as the king's daughter herself."

This wasn't a good path to follow. Dumphey nodded back toward the tools. "Well then, how…?" Dumphey couldn't voice his question.

Betin stood and rubbed the twine between his thumb and forefinger. "Algor was so close to his goal." He paused and dropped the twine. "'Twas justice he desired and hoped for. He worked for years." He ran his hand up and down the wood in his hands. "This wood is ready to be made into a bow, because of him."

So that was where Betin had obtained the bow he always kept with him. Lord Feroci dealt with weapons such as swords, spears, and javelins. Dumphey had never known of a bowyer in Abtshire.

"Bow material doesn't cure in mere days. It takes years—three years, four—before it is ready."

"He was able to hide this ability from Feroci?" A tiny ray of hope surged inside of Dumphey. If one man could keep out of the lord's sight for years, mayhap a group of lads had potential to do the same if they were watching out for each other.

"Feroci never discovered his work." Betin snapped the words out. He loosened his hold on the dagger and began cutting thin slivers of wood from the staff. "He didn't know what Algor was up to. Just rumors." His nostrils flared and his Adam's apple bobbed. He met Dumphey's gaze. "Algor was hung on rumors."

Dumphey's body stiffened as an image of Lia flashed through his mind. Because of God's mercy in sending Lord Kiralyn, she hadn't been hung, but he still couldn't erase the image of what could have happened. "'Tis injustice." Just like the accusations against him of murder. Had someone begun to circulate rumors about him that made the lord desire his death also? But why? For the mere act of providing for the peasants' needs? Surely the lord didn't plan on starving Abtshire to death? He shook the unpleasant thoughts from his mind and turned back to the conversation at hand. "But … they weren't just rumors, were they?"

"Not wholly." Betin focused his attention on his work. His hands deftly carved the wood, the discarded chips scattering to the ground. "He was guilty of nothing that Barat accused him, though. Algor was not leading a rebellion against the lord. Not exactly."

"Then what is the truth about Algor?" Dumphey couldn't squelch his curiosity. He had only heard from the soldiers how vile the man had been. He didn't know Algor, but he knew Betin. And surely such a kind, level-headed lad such as this couldn't have been under a man guilty of the accusations laid upon him.

Betin blew out a breath of air and set his staff aside. He leaned forward, elbows resting on his knees, his whole attention on Dumphey. "The lord isn't following the laws of the land."

Aye, this much Dumphey—and half of Abtshire—knew. Though no one dared speak such things in Abtshire's streets.

"Algor believed that Lord Feroci was working with a circle of lords who were attempting to overthrow King Jarin."

Dumphey froze. *Overthrow.* The word pierced through his memory. He had heard that word in connection with Lord Feroci recently. Where?

"Algor died trying to verify the rumor and report to the king."

Dumphey crouched down beside Betin. He swiped his clammy hands on his jerkin, not able to shake the thought that he knew something more than he realized. "He trained you to take his place." He didn't doubt it as he watched Betin grip the dagger again. Its blade flew expertly over the staff, creating angles that didn't make sense to Dumphey, but seemed to please Betin. "Betin, are you out for revenge?"

Betin's freckled face pulled tight in concentration as he ran his fingers over the wood he had just shaped. His movement was quick and sure. Finally, he spoke. "Not revenge. Vengeance is of the Lord." He paused again and took a deep breath. "Oh, how I wanted to. That eve when he hung. Every part of my being wanted to rush forward and kill Barat and the others. But such are not the ways of God."

"Why are you here, then?" Dumphey asked.

"Every man has a choice. He can choose blindness concerning the evil that surrounds him, or he can choose to make a difference. I am determined to be the latter man—to fight for justice in this land. Yet I must be patient until I can. Until I can do all in my power against Feroci."

"But not to kill him?" Dumphey tested Betin with a look.

Betin looked away, his voice a soft whisper. "Nay, 'twas never my intention." He swallowed and took a deep breath then turned back to Dumphey. "'Tis one of the disagreements we had with Cedric. He wanted to take aggressive action, I did not. But you are right. God hasn't allowed us to live in ease here without a cause. Mayhap He has placed us here for a reason—to help Abtshire in ways that no one else can." He stood to his feet and extended a hand to Dumphey. "And mayhap He led you here to be our leader—to be the level head that we need, yet willing to take the steps needed to work." Shame filled Betin's face even as Dumphey clasped his hand in a firm handshake. "I haven't the ability to say 'yea and nay' when needed."

Dumphey tamped down the questions that rose in his heart at this sudden offer from Betin. "'Twould be an honor but..." The memory of Lia's arrest and imprisonment flashed through his mind. When it came to confronting the evil directly, to being the one voice that spoke against a multitude of naysayers, he had failed. Added to that, he had bent under the pressure of a bribe for his personal benefit. "I don't believe that I am the right man for the job."

Betin squeezed his hand tighter. "I have watched you, Dumphey. I have heard your passion. You are guided by more than just your distaste for Feroci. Aye, I believe you are just the man."

Though his mouth went dry, Dumphey forced a smile. Had he not prayed earnestly this last year for opportunities to do more for Abtshire? More against Feroci? He ducked his head from Betin's intense stare and whispered, "I'll consider it."

Chapter Nine

$\mathcal{D}$umphey wrapped his fingers around the bow. It felt good. Much different than the leather thongs of his sling. It was powerful. Like a key beyond freedom—the one to victory.

"Well?" Betin asked.

"Have you an arrow?" Dumphey ran his fingers along the twine that suspended between the tips. Just a few days before, this had been but a stick. Betin worked wonders with his tools.

Betin grinned and removed an arrow from the quiver at his side. "I can lend you some for now." He held the arrows out to Dumphey. "But these are mine."

Dumphey gave him a grin, reached for the arrows, and placed it on his finger that was gripping the bow. "How am I so far?"

Betin gave a cocked smile. "About as well as any beginner, I'd say. Though if we were relying on you for dinner, I'd recommend the sling." He motioned for Dumphey to hand the bow over. He gripped the bow with his left hand and placed an arrow on the right side. Then, he paused. His green eyes pierced the forest like a hawk eying its prey.

"What—"

"Sh." It was more a motion than a sound. Betin waited a second more, then clicked his tongue. The slight movement beyond them stopped at the noise.

Dumphey followed Betin's gaze in time to see the arrow hit its target.

"We've dinner," Betin said. He eased forward, bow in hand.

Dumphey trailed behind him. Betin's muscles bulged beneath the thin layer of fabric as he moved without a sound.

"You've done this before," Dumphey said lightly. It felt good to be mirthful after spending long moments worrying over Betin's proposition. He had tried praying and fasting, seeking the Lord about whether or not to accept Betin's offer, but his past failures burned at him. He could almost hear Zuzene's gentle voice reminding him to forget those things which were behind and push toward those things before him. But if he didn't feel adequate guilt over his failures, he'd never be able to move forward. Finally, he had made the decision.

"Aye, I've done it once or twice." Betin winked as he handed the bow back to Dumphey and bent down to pick up the squirrel and arrow. "We'll need more than one of these if we're going to share—and keep Patey from stealing from the lord's larder."

All joviality ceased with those words. Though he had been respectful, Patey's response left Dumphey doubting that things would change anytime soon. One couldn't expect change to happen immediately, though. Dumphey had to be patient for the thought to take root in the hearts of all the lads. He had already won over Betin and Stefan. Arther may grumble, but he was agreed to it. 'Twould just be a matter of time before Dickie and Patey followed, content to use only the gleanings of the forest to care for a handful of peasants in Abtshire, rather than looting the lord's larder.

Dumphey nodded toward the squirrel Betin held. "I suppose that means my archery lesson gets delayed, for I would only scare the squirrels into hiding."

Betin grinned. "You're a fast learner." He tossed the squirrel into a second sack. He must have been planning a hunt all along. Betin's smile faded and his gaze turned searching. Dumphey knew what was coming next. "Have you an answer for me?"

Dumphey unwrapped his sling from his waist and slid his finger into the loop cord. "Aye."

Betin's brows shot upward. "Aye, you've an answer, or *aye*, you will do it?"

Dumphey grinned at the mix of confusion and hope blazoned on Betin's face. "Aye."

Betin's smile returned and he punched Dumphey on the shoulder.

"But only with your help," Dumphey said. "The lads respect you, Betin. I shan't discount that."

Betin nodded. "I shall be there. Now, for our first task—meat for as many in Abtshire as we can provide." He led the way, ducking under branches and looking around with each step. The lord's men usually stayed in the lowlands, but there were a few intense days when the lads had seen hints of yellow and red nearby. It now appeared as if the soldiers had turned to other things, but the lads were being cautious. As long as Dumphey and his friends stayed here, they had an advantage. But they couldn't afford to be careless. Their lives, and the lives of the peasants in Abtshire, counted on it.

Betin motioned for Dumphey to be still. Dumphey waited as Betin removed another arrow with ease and silence. If Dumphey hadn't been watching, he wouldn't have known when Betin made each change in position. The arrow slid through the air and hit its target. Betin may not be teaching Dumphey in words, but by observing, Dumphey was learning far more about the skill than had ever been permitted in Abtshire.

"Their tails will be invaluable to us." Betin pointed to the pieces of fur that were wrapped around the bowstring.

"They silence the release of the bow. If animals cannot hear the sound, neither can humans."

Dumphey nodded. "Do all the lads have weapons?"

"You're the last."

"What of extras? In case something goes awry or…" —heaven forbid— "Or we've others who need the protection of joining our group."

Betin grew thoughtful. "I like your way of thinking. The others can hunt. I've material to make enough bows and arrows for a small army." He shrugged. "Not that we need one today, but for whenever we decide to do more than feed the poor."

The implications were obvious, but Dumphey didn't comment. Helping the poor he could do. Taking on Lord Feroci's army? Dumphey had trained in the barracks. Shivers fingered across his shoulders. There were lads he knew and trusted at the barracks. What if they stayed true to Feroci and turned against Dumphey? 'Twould be madness to think that their small band of lads could be victorious over a hundred trained and armored men. *I pray, God, for Thy guidance every step of the way.* 'Twould be the only way they could move forward. If God would look past Dumphey's faults and guide him.

Betin nodded toward Dumphey's sling. "Show me what you can do."

Dumphey grinned and removed a cobble from his pocket. He felt its weight in the pouch as he scanned the forest for another squirrel—or mayhap he'd be lucky and see a hare, given his inaccuracy with the sapling not many days before. Betin touched his shoulder and pointed. Brown fur blended in with the leaves that lined the forest floor.

Dumphey swung the sling around then leaned forward and released. The cobble sped toward its target and bounced as it hit the ground. The squirrel disappeared in a heartbeat.

"'Tis well you're not relying on my skills for dinner," Dumphey said. "I can hit one in twenty tries. Now, if it were a man, I would have hit him for certain." Not that he had ever tried before. As far as anyone in Abtshire knew, the rope wrapped around his waist was but a belt. He retrieved his stone and returned it to his pouch. "This is why we need bows and arrows, not slings—for our sustenance as well as defense."

Betin grinned. "Your sling is still impressive, though."

"'Twas the only thing I could practice in secret." Dumphey looked out, alert for any movement around him. In the distance, something skittered down a tree. He touched Betin's arm and pointed. Two more squirrels would suffice for a dinner fit for the lord's courts. The thought made Dumphey's mouth water in anticipation. He still hadn't gotten used to their free access to food. Aye, 'twas only right to share this goodness with others.

Betin stood still and drew back the bow. The arrow flew through the air and Betin gave a slight nod. "Nice eye," he said. "Now…" He unlaced his wrist guard then held out the bow to Dumphey. "Your turn."

Dumphey tied the leather guard on his left arm then let the heaviness of the bow settle in his hands. He pulled back the string, testing the weight of the draw, before notching an arrow.

"Just hit a tree. If you can." Slight amusement tinged Betin's words.

Dumphey mimicked the stance he had seen in Betin and drew back. A scraggly pine, no wider than Dumphey's hand, stood about sixty paces away. Shoulders squared and feet planted, he pulled back and aimed. A burst of power pulsed through his body as the arrow released. It stuck the tree. Dead center.

"Again!" Betin had an arrow held out and ready.

Dumphey took it in silence. He aimed above his other arrow and shot. Bark splintered as the arrow embedded into the tree. Center, again. Dumphey schooled back a smile and refrained from running forward to pluck the arrows from the tree. He glanced over at Betin. The lad was slowly shaking his head as he reached for another arrow.

"I don't believe this," Betin said.

The arrow was smooth and calming in Dumphey's palm. He rolled it between his fingers before sliding it onto the bow.

"If you hit center thrice, these arrows are yours."

Dumphey angled a smile toward Betin. "Dost thou attempt to throw me off target with thy challenge?"

Betin threw his hands up in defense. "Nay! I am astounded. You promise you've never touched a bow?"

Dumphey shook his head. "The only weapon I have is my sling." He guided his attention back to the tree and aimed. Between the two arrows was his goal. He held his breath and released the arrow. It landed squarely between the other two, slightly closer to the top arrow.

Betin gave a low whistle. "'Tis yours, Dumphey. I suppose I must get to work and create some replacements."

Dumphey walked forward, his muscles taut as he pulled out the three arrows. He could aim, aye, but if he was going to last in battle, he needed to get used to the exertion.

Excitement coursed through his veins like a torrent of rain in drought. "Keep your arrows, Betin. But make mine posthaste." He held out the arrows to Betin. Instead of taking them, Betin pressed his hand over Dumphey's fist holding the arrows.

"There are moments like these, when it feels like success is but a handbreadth away."

Dumphey nodded. Armed and equipped, they could do so much more than he had ever dared dream of while in Abtshire. He opened his mouth to speak but was interrupted with the crack of a stick. Someone was coming.

Chapter Ten

ord Feroci's men had captured a group of lads from the forest—to be hung at dawn. Noel's fingers fumbled as they straightened the tack on the walls, readying it for the morrow. No matter how much he tried to convince himself—no matter how hard he prayed—he could not ease the fear that it was Patey and Dumphey's group. There was no other band so brave as to attempt to hide away from the lord in the forest. And because it wasn't Patey who had shared the news, but a young lass, it only intensified the alarm that surged through Noel's whole being. 'Twould seem a simple task to leave the shelter of the stables and walk to the other side of the barracks to see for himself, but the thought of weaving between a dozen soldiers paralyzed Noel.

Father above, protect Dumphey, and spare his life. His hands trembled as the thought charged through him again: what would he do, if his brother were slain? What *could* he do? His breath caught in his throat.

"Working late, I see." Philaon stepped beside Noel and watched him a moment. "You needn't worry about taking up double tasks for your brother. We've been able to carry our load sufficiently without him."

If only that were the cause of his busy hands.

"The lord is about to bring in more horses." Philaon sighed and Noel noticed the heavy lines that creased across his forehead. He was only a couple years older than Dumphey, but in this moment, he looked a decade older. "It's taken work, but he's agreed for another stable hand."

Noel looked up, his eyes wide. "Lord Feroci allowed that?" Though the lord kept the fields flush with workers, when it came to the care of his horses, he expected few hands to be multiplied by sheer desire. Or so, Dumphey had said.

Philaon shrugged. "There is work to be done, and he told me that he cared not how it was done; 'tis my responsibility." His shoulders sagged as he bent to pick up a halter that had fallen to the ground.

"I apologize for the trouble my brother has put you in," Noel said. He suspected that since Dumphey had been connected with the stables, even Philaon was under scrutiny.

The stable master waved the apology aside. "I realize you are not responsible for Dumphey's choices. But I would advise you not to follow in his footsteps."

"Aye." Noel returned to brushing the tack as his stomach clenched. Especially if those footsteps led him to the gallows.

"I trust you will show the new lass the ways of the stables. But let it not interfere with completing tasks done in time. Barat already has his eye on you."

Noel swallowed as Philaon walked deeper into the stables. 'Twas a kindly warning, but it struck fear into the core of his heart. After rumors of Dumphey's theft and murder, a stronger guard unit had been stationed around the stables. Many times, Noel had felt the eyes of soldiers watching him as he walked around Abtshire. He never ventured further than necessary to carry on his duties.

He entered the stall of a horse that had gotten a cut last night in the lord's excursion. 'Twas one of the lord's favorites, so the horse wouldn't be given much rest before being used again—even if Philaon dared mention the injury to Lord Feroci.

Noel brought the horse to the center and tied him to a pole then placed a bucket of feed in front to keep the horse occupied while he cleaned and applied salve to the cut. As he walked to get a water bucket, the stable door opened again. Noel's muscles tensed even as he made a conscious effort to ignore whoever was entering the stables. If the lord sent men to interrogate him of his brother, he had no answers.

"You must be Noel."

Noel looked up into the eyes of a lass who was near his own height, her hair brown with a reddish tint, her eyes green. She was likely close to Dumphey's age.

"Aye, I'm Noel." This must be the extra help Philaon had mentioned, for what other lass would wander into the stables under the guards' noses? "Who is asking?"

"'Tis Lydda." She looked at Noel with a serious expression. "I am told you are to be my tutor in the ways of stable life."

Noel glanced down the stables for Philaon, but the stable master was nowhere in sight. "I suppose I am. Know you anything of horses?"

"My father owned a horse here. Before..." she lowered her voice, "before he passed."

Noel winced. Such sorrow had touched the lives of every lad and lass in Abtshire. When would it cease? He glanced beyond Lydda to the fading light outside the stables. Would it be his turn to embrace such sorrow on the morn? He choked out, "I'm sorry for your loss."

Lydda shrugged her thin shoulders. "Years have healed the sorrow somewhat." Yet the weariness on her face told that she was lying—like so many in Abtshire were forced to do.

She motioned toward the stalls. "I cannot help every moment. I work in the candle maker's shop during the day."

Like Lia, Lydda was a lass who was attempting to carry two large tasks. Noel knew that she wouldn't step away from this, even if he voiced his concerns. "Follow me." He led her to the tack and picked up a harness. "I've already done these." He had intended to return to the rest and finish after he cared for the injured horse. If Lydda did them, he'd muck out the stalls. "The lord is very particular about clean tack. 'Tis leather, so you must take care—"

"Aye, I know the workings of leather," Lydda said. The thoughtful look that had come across her face convinced Noel.

Shame filled him for assuming the lass ignorant. He stuttered out, "Then… then you are well-suited for this task."

Lydda's lips turned up as if she were assuring him it was all right. But in the next second, the moment of ease faded and she leaned closer. "Is it true that your brother is part of the band leading a rebellion against the lord and his men?"

A chill settled on Noel's back. Had Lord Feroci sent Lydda here to spy on him and learn his motives? Or to give report of Noel's knowledge? He suppressed a shudder. From whence came these suspicious thoughts and doubt of others' character? Yet any thoughts Noel had of finding the location of the imprisoned group fled his mind. What had he been thinking? The lord would have double-guards on duty tonight. Was there anyone in Abtshire he could trust? He turned his back on Lydda and said, "My brother left days ago. I know not his intent or where he is now."

"Very well." Lydda's voice was a whisper.

Noel left her to her task and walked numbly back to the injured horse. How long would he be safe, if one of Feroci's spies was in his presence? He bent down to rinse the horse's leg and stole a glance at Lydda as she put her full attention to her task. Noel tried to tamp down his fears with prayers, but one thought prevailed: if Patey wasn't captured and he came again, 'twould only mean trouble for the both of them.

Chapter Eleven

$\mathcal{D}$umphey's skin crawled and his throat tightened from dryness as he glanced at the gallows silhouetted against the night's dimness. Between the gallows and the barracks, the lads were secured to a tree. Betin shifted beside him. 'Twas Dumphey's decision to come here. Betin had backed his choice, but Dickie had cackled louder than a hen whose eggs were stolen from her. There were lives in danger, though. And it didn't matter that it was Cedric and the lads he had led away from the safety of Betin's group—they didn't deserve to die at the whim of Feroci.

"He wishes to make an example of them," Patey had said.

An example for whom? The villagers in Abtshire who were too fearful to venture beyond the guarded perimeter?

Or an example to Dumphey, Betin, and their faithful lads? If the latter, then why in Abtshire? With the far-fetched hope that word would return to the forest of these lads' demise? Dumphey's fingers pulsed as they clenched his bow. Betin had made fast work of creating more arrows— but would they be enough for their patchwork plan?

Feroci wouldn't suspect someone coming tonight. At least, 'twas what Patey had assured him. Nothing of this sort had ever taken place in Abtshire before—if the lord made plans, they were executed without interruption. Except for tonight. Dumphey prayed things would change tonight. Only three guards stood between the gallows and the tree, the yellow on their quilted doublets standing out in the darkness.

Dumphey notched an arrow and played with the bowstring's tension. Zuzene had often said not to tempt God—Dumphey hoped relying on his bow before he had fully tested it wasn't one of those instances. Or maybe it was tempting God by tackling this before he had settled in his heart the issue of the bribery.

But things felt right, and they were doing a good deed. Dickie had scoffed at his inexperience, but Dumphey ignored him, praying that God would look beyond their faults and provide help. They desperately needed it.

"Let me cut their bonds," Patey whispered.

Dumphey caught himself before leaping at Patey's sudden approach.

Betin cast him a glare that was only half-hidden by the night's shadows. "Nay. We haven't another in Abtshire to replace your work here. If this fails, and Feroci sees you…" his voice trailed off and Dumphey could fill in the blanks all too well.

"If this fails, ye will have no need of me," Patey said, his tone cocky.

"Our families do!" Betin hissed.

Dumphey stepped up. If Patey got more agitated, he would blow their cover. "Dickie is already sneaking around to do it. To change plans now would be disastrous." And they didn't need anything to be disastrous. He still doubted his choice to put Dickie on the task. The lad was limber and quick, but over-confidence often led to carelessness. "Patey, we need you to return to your abode. If Feroci is beginning to suspect you, we need to throw him off track."

Patey stood silent for a long moment—doubtless rolling retorts in his mind. But he turned and left, so silently that if Dumphey hadn't seen the shadow move, he wouldn't have known. Aye, Patey was too good an asset to their band to be discovered yet.

Betin sighed, likely with the same relief that Dumphey felt. "Are we ready?"

Dumphey hoped so. Prayed so. Even though he had his doubts, energy surged through him. Though he had been with the lads but a few days, they were a tight-knit clan. Or so he wanted to believe. Tonight would be a test of that.

He took a step beyond the cottage that was hiding them. If only the uncompleted barracks was hidden from the castle's view. He was but a stone's throw from the castle. Lord Feroci may not be expecting company tonight, but he wasn't foolish in his planning.

Dumphey crouched and hurried forward, his footsteps quiet on the cobbled ground, away from the scene of the prisoners. He was just a few paces from the castle, with Betin near behind. A clipped footstep froze Dumphey in place. A soldier rounded the corner of the castle. Betin's eyes asked the question and Dumphey gave a slight nod. In a swift movement, Betin was on the soldier's back, one arm around the man's throat and his hand clamped over his mouth. Dumphey slung his bow over his shoulder, leapt forward, and gripped the soldier's thrashing arms to keep him from drawing a weapon. In a moment, the soldier was still. The lads eased him to the ground then disarmed him. Dumphey tied the soldier while Betin shoved a wadded cloth in his mouth. They hid him in the shadows where someone would find him in the morn.

Heart pounding, Dumphey secured the soldier's belt and dagger around his own waist then found his bow. He turned away from the castle and faced the barracks. He pulled the bow back into his hands. If time demanded him to act quickly with his weapon, could he do it? He crouched even lower and slowed his pace. The guards' backs were to him. They were tall, rigid, and—Dumphey could only assume—alert.

Cedric and the lads were tied to the one tree the Lord Feroci had left by the barracks. Dumphey hoped it was only part of the "public show" Feroci had planned.

Father God, help us tonight. He looked beyond the guards and squinted until he could make out a form separated from the barracks—now creeping toward the tree that held the prisoners. The guards needed to be distracted. He felt Betin move beside him. A cobble tripped in front of him. He held his hand out to Betin and hissed a "Shh!" Too late, he realized his error. The guards were distracted, all right. Just at the wrong time.

They spun, their maille armor pounding in the silence.

"Who goes there?"

Dumphey flattened against the ground, his hands ready to leverage him at a moment's notice. *Make your move now, Dickie.* If it was Patey, the lad would be at the tree, doing his work.

"Eh, jumpy tonight, are ye, Symeon?"

"Hold your tongue. I know I heard someone." The speaker took a step forward.

Dumphey fought against the urge to slide backward. He held his breath, fearing even the movement of filling his lungs would give them away.

"No one's out this time of night. They wouldna want the fee." A different guard spoke this time.

Still, all three were facing Dumphey and Betin.

"Get a torch."

No! It was all Dumphey could do to keep from scrambling at the suggestion.

"You get a torch yourself. I didna hear anything."

Dumphey tried to focus beyond the guards to any activity behind them, but the distance was too great to see through the shadows. *Hurry, Dickie.* He had Dumphey's dagger. All that was needed was a few swift cuts, a few whispered directions, then Cedric and the others would be safely with Arther and Stefan.

"Run." Betin's hushed warning severed Dumphey's focus from Dickie's responsibility to the soldiers—who were now near enough for Dumphey to reach out with his bow and touch. Adrenaline coursed through him and he leapt to his feet.

"Halt!"

Dumphey was close on Betin's heels. He followed as Betin wove his way through the empty streets of Commerce Row, not caring how loudly his feet clambered now. They were already discovered. His head throbbed as he scanned the area. Dark streets led to more dark streets.

"You keep on." Dumphey tried to keep his voice low, yet loud enough for Betin to hear. He looked over his shoulder. There were only two soldiers now. He clenched his teeth and darted to the left, between two cottages. And plowed into a wall of armor.

Chapter Twelve

Strong arms wrapped around Dumphey then squeezed. Dumphey struggled as a solid forearm slammed against his throat then tightened. Dark splotches floated in Dumphey's vision.

"Ho there!" a distant voice exclaimed.

The grip loosened and Dumphey drilled one of his arrows into the exposed part of the soldier's leg. The hold on him released completely and Dumphey fell to the ground. He heard a sword unsheathe and scrambled backward. He was too close to use his bow. He fumbled for the dagger at his waist.

A whistle split the air. This time, nearer than the shout.

"If ye want a duel, sir, come here." The voice was strangely accented, but Dumphey detected a familiar undertone.

Patey wasn't supposed to be here. Relief surged through Dumphey as the soldier spun from him and faced the lad. Except Patey was no longer there. Dumphey struggled to his feet and positioned his arrow as Patey gave another taunt. He heard nothing of Betin and the other soldiers. He could only pray that Betin made it out better than him.

A voice whispered behind Dumphey, "Take your leave." Then Patey tossed a pebble toward the other side of the guard.

"What? For you to face him alone?"

"Sh. He doesn't know who I am—or where. Just go." Patey raised his voice as he ran away from Dumphey. "Over yonder, my good sir."

Dumphey used Patey's exclamation as his cover and crept back toward the street. All was still and silent. He moved with as much speed as he dared, threading his way through Abtshire. The soldiers must not have sounded an alarm, because Feroci's guard wasn't ravaging the streets. Odd. Where were they?

Dumphey slowed as he neared the edge of Abtshire. If separated, he and Betin had agreed to meet on the north side of town, near the king's highway. 'Twould take extra time to go there from Commerce Row, but Dumphey couldn't leave Betin alone. He kept in the trees and circled around Abtshire until he reached the king's highway. The moon cast its dim glow on the road. Six trees down then six trees into the forest was where they'd meet—one for every lad in their group, making the number easy to remember. Dumphey started toward the place when a sound made him freeze. There was nothing. His mind was tricking him. Too much had happened this night, making him jumpy. Still, he looked fully around him to be certain.

A mass of guards crowded the entrance to the castle and flanked out into the king's highway. Dumphey crouched down and counted. There were well over three dozen. He leaned forward. Five or six, he could understand, but so many? Why?

The breeze blew, rustling leaves and branches above him. The low call of a night bird blended with the breeze. 'Twas an imitation. A good one. One that only Betin could make. Dumphey waited as the wind died down then picked up again before he gave a soft reply. He didn't know where Betin was, but the lad had practice in tracking calls. Within minutes, Dumphey heard someone approaching—only because he was listening carefully for it.

Betin crouched beside him, facing the row of guards.

"What are they up to?" Dumphey asked.

His friend sighed. The one sound said nothing and everything. He didn't know, but he had too many suspicions.

"This is why 'twas so easy to get into Abtshire tonight," Dumphey said. He backed away from the opening in the trees that gave a clear view of the castle and stepped cautiously away from Abtshire.

"Methinks they're waiting for someone," Betin whispered when they were a few paces away.

"But who?"

Betin took a few quick steps until he was in front of Dumphey then stopped. "We need to find out. This is linked to what Algor was finding. I'm certain of it."

Dumphey hesitated. That one word came to mind again: overthrow. He closed his eyes and tried to bring it fully to surface. It seemed further in the distance than when Betin had mentioned it the other day.

"Let us at least see." Without waiting for an answer, Betin changed direction and walked parallel to the king's highway.

They traveled in silence for a long while. Dumphey refused to let his mind settle on any one thing as they walked. The danger behind them, the danger before them, the danger of the other lads—or the unknown danger of Feroci's plans. His mind froze. Aye, that was where he had heard the word. Feroci. What had he heard, though? And when?

He tried to pray, but his senses were too distracted by studying everything around him. Every few paces, they would stop just to listen. Usually, only the sounds of the night air welcomed them. But this time when they stopped, there was something else in the distance—a steady rhythm.

"A horse," Betin said, verifying Dumphey's thoughts.

Dumphey quickened his pace beside Betin. The next time they paused, the hoof beats had stopped.

"Where did he go?" Dumphey asked.

Betin made a sound in his throat and stepped closer to the highway. They were well out of sight of Abtshire by now—out of hearing range as well. Gradually, Dumphey heard another sound. It wasn't as loud as hoof beats. He looked as far as he dared onto the king's highway. There. A lone man was walking toward them, slowly and steadily.

"What I thought," Betin said.

'Twasn't a soldier clad in armor. Rather, his dark clothing was meant to blend into the shadows. A messenger. A secret messenger.

Dumphey pulled three arrows from his quiver. "We shoot as rapidly as we can—just at his feet to confuse him. Then we find what he has."

Betin tilted his head in silent agreement. They waited until the figure was about ten paces beyond them. Dumphey drew an arrow and Betin followed his lead. They released within seconds of each other then drew and released again. Instead of crying out, the man drew something from his belt and leapt into the grove of trees opposite.

"After him!" Betin bent and picked up their arrows as he crossed the highway.

Branches snapped, giving them a clear path to pursue their messenger. Dumphey created a slight distance between him and Betin, hoping they could cut the man off from his straight path.

The noise ahead of him stopped. Dumphey held his bow and arrow at the ready and slowed until he was barely making progress. He studied the shadows ahead of him. For a brief moment, he caught a movement just two paces in front of him. Then, the shadow moved—toward him. Dumphey wielded his bow as a sword and slammed it into the man.

Movement flashed beside Dumphey and Betin landed on top of the man. "Give me a hand, will you?"

Dumphey tossed his weapon aside, untied his belt, then wrapped it around the hands that Betin was fighting to hold still.

"To your feet, man." Betin jerked him up as he spoke.

Dumphey tried to evaluate the man in the darkness. He stood almost calmly as Betin patted him down, searching.

"A second dagger." Betin tossed it aside. "And a third." He added it to the pile.

Dumphey folded his arms as he watched. "I don't suppose you'd be so kind as to tell us the amount of daggers we're searching for, aye?"

He could feel the man's glare on him.

"Anything besides daggers you might be carrying?"

"Mayhap this." Betin handed Dumphey a small sack.

Dumphey thumbed through it. "Two coins and stale clap-bread. Not much use." He fingered the seams, searching for a hidden pocket. Nothing.

"Four daggers. I suppose 'tis a good plan to have so many, traveling this late at night."

"But why traveling this late at night?" And with an embassy awaiting him in Abtshire? The man hadn't fought hard to use his daggers in defense. He acted too much like there was nothing to hide. If Dumphey were carrying a sensitive missive, where would he keep it?

"Check his shoes," Dumphey said.

'Twas hard to tell in the shadows, but Dumphey thought he saw the man shift positions. He knelt beside Betin and reached for the man's shoe. A sharp blow rammed his cheek, throwing him backward. He regained his balance as Betin tackled the man to the ground.

"Methinks you hit a sore spot." Betin grunted as he wrestled with the man.

"Methinks he *gave* a sore spot." Dumphey lunged for the man's legs. He hung onto one, bracing himself against the blows of the other foot as he jerked off the shoe. He tossed it beside the daggers, reached for the other foot, wrenched the shoe off, and leapt away from the kicking.

Betin gave a few grunts, then the tussle ceased.

"You owe me for that one."

Betin took one of the shoes and examined it.

"I owe *you*?" Dumphey worked his jaw as he shoved the daggers inside one of the shoes.

"Aye." Betin thumped the sole of the shoe. "Definitely a false bottom."

As much as Dumphey suspected. "Let's get out before he wakes." They could check the shoes later for the missive.

"When Feroci discovers this…" Betin took off to a run. "We must go into secure hiding. Follow me."

Chapter Thirteen

Noel squinted in the sunlight after emerging from the dungeon. Visits to Zuzene usually lifted his spirits, but not today. She had asked after Dumphey, of course, but he had nothing to report. Guilt tore at his every step as he walked past the soldier who guarded the dungeon entrance. He should have gone last evening—he should have been there when Dumphey needed him. But he hadn't been. Nothing had been said of the lads who were to be hung. Rumors were confounding. First, he heard that the lads had escaped—every last one of them. But close on the heels of that rumor was that the lord had postponed their execution. Which was then followed by the assumption that Lord Feroci had taken them to the forest to execute them.

Patey was nowhere to be seen, which both relieved and perplexed Noel. Every time Patey visited, he felt the rising suspicion of the soldiers shadowing his path. But without Patey, he had heard nothing of his brother in days. Even Barat hadn't been around to interrogate him. Surely... surely if one of the lads was Dumphey, the magnate would have found his way to the stables? The whole thing gave Noel an empty feeling in the pit of his stomach.

He wove his way through the streets, his bare feet stirring up clouds of dust as he walked. 'Twas near harvest-time. The daylight hours were fewer, and the wind colder. Everywhere he went was the hushed discussion of the peasants, bemoaning the small crops of this year's upcoming harvest. Fear gnawed at Noel's bones. 'Twould be a harsh winter for Abtshire. He was certain of it.

Noel turned and caught the glare of a fully-armored guard with a red and yellow cloak. His heart pounded and he set off at a quick pace toward the stables. Dumphey's disappearance—aye, maybe 'twas two disappearances now—put a broad target on Noel's back. He was sure that the entire army had been warned to keep an eye on him and his actions.

I shall have to act with even greater caution. Had not the believers in the new assembly, soon after Jesus' resurrection, done the same? Noel would have to ask Zuzene to tell him the story once more. It encouraged him, thinking of how holy men and women of old had faced hardship yet had not done so at the cost of following God. 'Twas possible to do both—follow God and live uprightly in hard times—of that he was certain.

But how could he do so today?

He braced himself as he entered the stables. He never knew what he would face inside these doors. Barat. A band of soldiers. Lydda. The latter hadn't given him reason to suspect a pact with the lord, but her actions were always shaded with something that Noel couldn't discern.

Philaon looked up from the workhorse he was leading out of a stall when Noel entered. "'Tis time you returned. Lydda was seeking you." His face drew into a frown. "You ought to be available to train her at all times. 'Twill keep us from trouble with the lord."

Noel nodded stiffly. "I'm sorry, sir."

"Barat ordered for you to get twelve horses armored." He nodded toward the mounts that were already stationed in the back of the stable, ready for their tack.

Armored? The racing of Noel's heart only increased, throbbing with hope that the rumors of Dumphey's escape were actually true. "Did he say why?"

Philaon ran a finger along the bridle of the horse he held. "Does our station ever get a reason why we must do our tasks?" For that one moment, Noel saw him not as the young man he looked up to, but a lad near his brother's age, his heart just as much at a loss to do good as his own. "Nay. The lord has his own plans, and they must not be questioned."

103

A stone settled in Noel's stomach like a warning sign. "Did he say how soon the lord would be expecting them?"

"In an hour." Philaon gave Noel a look that hinted at pity as he took the reins of a second workhorse. "I tarried to tell you. I would help if I could, but the lord is waiting for more workhorses at the barracks."

An hour. For twelve, fully-armored horses. Surely Philaon knew 'twas a nigh impossible task for one to do alone. His eyes slid shut and he sucked in a breath of air. 'Twas one thing to ask his brother for assistance. Quite another to ask Lydda. Especially if she was working for the lord and spying on Noel.

There were some pieces of the maille that he could attach without assistance. He had watched Dumphey do it many times. He filled his hands with the cool metal armor and braced himself as he lifted it. When he came to the horse, hands reached out and helped him hoist the armor over the horse's back.

"I cannot help you for long." Lydda's voice was low, but decisive. "Barat has ordered his own horse brought to him at the castle. I dare not push his patience." The way she looked over her shoulder made Noel wish he were as big and brave as Dumphey. Dumphey would do all he could to help the lass instead of expecting her to help him. Noel's stomach knotted. But Dumphey wasn't here. He didn't know where he was—or if he were even still alive.

Noel shifted the armor so that it flowed smoothly

down the horse's rear legs. He glanced at Lydda, but the lass was working on the other side and did not meet his gaze.

"I understand," he said. "If you can tarry long enough to help me with the largest pieces, I can do the rest."

Lydda nodded, and the two worked together in silence. As soon as the crupper and peytral were secure on the horses' flanks and shoulders, Lydda rested her hand on the horse's back and met Noel's gaze. The way she panted after these few moments of exertion jerked Noel's attention from his task. Again, he saw a glimpse of Lia—a lass taking on tasks more than her health allowed. He opened his mouth to beg her to consider leaving the stables, when she spoke.

"I believe your brother knows my brother."

The words sliced through Noel like an ax cutting wood—swift, hard, and thorough. He tightened the tail piece of the armor and released a sigh. Half the horses were left to complete. He went to the horse's head and draped the crinet over the mane. He didn't know what to say in response to Lydda. Dumphey may know her brother, or Lydda may be making things up to please the lord. Even if she was being honest. Even if he did know her brother, talking here—or anywhere in Abtshire— could be dangerous.

Lydda shuffled her feet and he glanced at her. "Please, you must let me know if Betin is safe." The words were soft, yet embraced with fear.

Betin? Noel moved to the next horse and tied the tail piece. Aye, he had heard the name, but he didn't know the fellow. He grabbed another crinet and walked to the second to last horse.

"Please." Lydda clenched her hand around Noel's forearm.

Noel turned to her. "I cannot speak now. Both you and I have tasks. Barat has ordered the horses—"

"Aye! The horses which he could very well send after my brother and yours!"

Noel clenched his jaw and smoothed the crinet over the mane, his fingers trembling as they worked in haste. "I cannot prevent that from happening." He hated himself, even as he said the words. He was nothing but a coward, bowing to the will of those stronger than he. Aye, he had thought himself strong when Dumphey was by his side. But now that it was just himself, he knew who he truly was. He cleared his throat. "Barat already suspects me to be privy to Dumphey and the others' works."

"You're not?" Lydda asked, her voice low and tremulous.

Noel glanced at her and shook his head. "Nay." He looked over the horse's body. He opened his mouth to add more when the stables door flung open in a way that only one person could make it. He swallowed. Barat was here, and he had no excuse.

Chapter Fourteen

The night air was cool and damp. Everything about Noel was scratchy and uncomfortable. His arms had lost all feeling just a few hours into the night. His legs were now tingling and growing numb. He tried to move his fingers, but the angle of the stocks made it difficult. He had seen many a peasant in the stocks and had always pitied them. Now that he was here—his arms secured up by his head and his legs tied securely under him—he knew that in the future he'd find ways to help those condemned to such injustice. At least bring them water to ease one area of suffering.

He focused his attention on the guard in front of them. It had been just a few minutes since the guard shift changed, but unlike the last guard, this one didn't appear interested in keeping his prisoners quiet. Instead, he drank freely from a jug, which Noel suspected held the lord's ale.

Noel prayed once more for Dumphey's protection—if he was still alive—and for Philaon to be shielded from the anger of Barat or the lord. 'Twasn't Philaon's fault that Noel had been caring for Zuzene, making him seem to neglect the order for the horses. At one time, Lord Feroci had freely granted permission for Noel to visit Zuzene. Apparently, he had withheld his favor without telling Noel.

Noel looked back at the guard. It had been a while since the jug had slipped to the ground. The guard's chin dropped down and rested on the yellow doublet covering his chest.

"Lydda?" Noel whispered, not taking his eyes off the guard.

"Hmm?" It was more of a moan than a question and irritated a weak cough from Lydda.

"I am terribly sorry you were brought into this." What was it Dumphey used to tell Lia? Stable work wasn't for a lass? He groaned. "I should have refused—"

"Shh…" Lydda sounded more alert now. "How many times need I tell you 'tisn't your fault? Lord Feroci will do what he wants to with any of us."

"But if you hadn't been helping me instead of tending to Barat's commands. If I hadn't stayed so long with Zuzene. Or if—"

"Hush, Noel. We must move beyond what has happened."

Noel took a breath. The night air coursed through his dry throat and rattled his lungs. He coughed, but it came out weak and led to another cough. He held his breath for a second then released it slowly. "What do you mean move beyond?"

"We must find Dumphey and Betin." Lydda's voice was soft, yet she spoke with determination. "We must work together with them. There is strength in numbers."

"I can't join Dumphey."

Lydda was silent as Noel carefully breathed in and out a few times. Then, she gave a hoarse, "What?"

Noel's leg muscles spasmed and he winced. Dumphey expected him to stay here and see that things were in order with helping the poor of Abtshire. If Dumphey wanted him, he would have sent for him by now. Even then, Noel wasn't sure he could leave his tasks at the stables undone. "I can't do as he does."

"What does he do?"

There. He had already said too much. "I—I don't know all."

"But what do you know?"

Noel tried to wriggle his fingers again, and pain shot through his arm. Tomorrow would be a miserable day of work after tonight—if Barat released him at dawn, as was the law of the land. Noel wasn't going to cling to that hope.

"Please, Noel."

He tried to look the direction of Lydda, but his head was too secure to move. The words that Patey had said that first night echoed in his mind—he had repeated them over and over until they were more familiar to him than his own thoughts—action, payback for cruelty. He had worried what that might mean. "I just want to be sure I'm following God and His ways."

"Well, I don't know about Dumphey, but Betin..." Lydda's voice went from uncertainty to anger. "I know my brother, and he would never do something against God."

"I don't know for certain." It sounded weak. Noel tried to shake his head, but the stocks held him secure. "Patey has boasted of what he's done. He says Dumphey is their new leader and that they plan to make a change in the land. After last night..." How he wished he could just speak with Dumphey once more, and clear away the fog of the rumors. "I fear for him, Lydda."

"Then..." Lydda paused as if she was searching for the right words to say. "What would you do, were you to do anything you wanted here?"

The air around Noel thickened with anticipation. He glanced toward the guard to be sure he was still asleep before answering, "I would be sure that no child in Abtshire goes to bed without food. That none of the peasants of Abtshire were punished unjustly. That every task would be repaid as is due instead of each soul taken advantage of." He let the words fall into the night air. So much hope bottled up now sounded impossible when spoken aloud. "I suppose it sounds foolish to dream of such for Abtshire."

"Nay." Lydda's voice was soft and gentle, bringing Noel back to the time when Mother was still alive, listening to him pour out his heart when Dumphey had suppressed his ideas with truths of reality.

Noel cleared his throat. "I'm naught but a stable boy. What can I do?"

"Surely we can do something."

We? Noel wished he could look at Lydda as she spoke.

"Well... we can pray."

Since Dumphey had left, Noel's prayers had been shortened as the workdays at the stables required more time. He let his neck rest against the rough wood of the stocks. Splinters cut into his flesh. Aye, he deserved to be here when he had so often failed to go to God. In doing so, he had failed the village and all he loved. He blinked back tears. *Father, forgive me. I have become wrapped up in the cares of this world and have not been seeking Thee and praying for others as I ought.* He would begin now. Names and faces raced through his mind—the miller, the candle maker, Zuzene, Philaon, Dumphey... An image of Barat and Lord Feroci flashed in Noel's mind. Months ago, he had regularly included them in his prayers, like Zuzene had said—praying for those in authority.

"Mayhap God will use people like Dumphey, Betin, you and I, as an answer to our prayers."

Noel jerked his attention back to Lydda. "Not if we try to rebel against authority. God is the One Who places men in authority, the One Who can change leaders' hearts."

"Aye," Lydda said. "Yet think of men of old, how God *used* them. He uses men—and women—on their knees, yet does He not use people in everyday life as well?"

Noel didn't have to think far to recall the tales of David, of Abraham, Job, Daniel, Paul, Nehemiah, Peter, and others God had used in the past.

"There is a time to pray and a time to follow God's leading and do something more. It doesn't mean we are seeking Him any less, does it?"

Noel closed his eyes. He could recount Zuzene's words best this way—as if he were in the darkness of the dungeon. Daniel, known as a man of faithful prayer, was also a man who had stood before the king.

The king! Noel's eyes flew open. Lord Kiralyn had said that he was kin to the king. And the king had no knowledge of the lord's unlawful government of Abtshire. He wouldn't know unless someone told him. If Noel could only reach Lia, she would believe him.

But Noel wasn't that someone. God may have chosen the shepherd-boy David to slay Goliath, but why would He send someone like Noel to the king? Chills broke out on Noel's skin. He would have to break the lord's laws in order to leave Abtshire and tell Lia. And if he was caught... 'twould be more than the stocks for him.

"Noel?"

Noel swallowed and licked his dry lips. "Aye?"

"Are you certain you know nothing of Betin?"

"Patey came to me…" Noel worked his jaw to keep the tightness from his words. "He refused to let me go to Dumphey. But I do know that Betin is with him."

"But he is well?"

Noel swallowed. If only he could reassure her of such. "I know they live in the forest. That they are working together."

A rustle sounded beside Noel. He strained to look, but could see nothing. "Finally, we've some direction. Well done, my good lass." Lord Feroci's voice broke the morning stillness like a scream piercing the calm.

Noel's neck cracked as he jerked it to try to glance at Lydda. His eyes stung from tears at the pain. Here he thought she was helping him—was sorrowing after her brother, just like him. But she was the lord's lackey after all?

"I think we can get more out of you, my lovelies. Alret!"

The guard jumped awake and stood before the lord.

Lord Feroci bent until his face was before Noel's. "I think we need to make a public show this morn."

Chapter Fifteen

*D*im light glowed from the embers of the small fire that Betin had lit. 'Twas a cave that Dumphey had heard nothing of in all the days he had been with the band, yet all the lads knew of it. Dumphey clasped the fingers of one hand in the other, willing warmth into them. Betin had kept the fire barely more than a bed of coals, almost not enough to call it an actual fire.

They had joined up with Stefan, Arther, and Dickie the night before and spent yesterday moving their camp here. They had a narrow escape. Only by the grace of God had they made it back to the forest with everyone.

Dumphey tamped down the bitterness that wanted to swell in his chest. It hadn't even been daybreak when Cedric, Simon, Luther, and William had left again. This time, thieving from the ones who had rescued them—

taking some foodstuff and weapons. Not all their weapons, granted. Each lad had slept with his own—they never rested without a bit of security lest something befall them. Dumphey hadn't wanted the belligerent lads to stick around, but what gratitude was that?

He turned his mind away from the lads, hoping he'd not have to see them again. That was this morning; nightfall was here again. Betin was right about the messenger. They had spent a good portion of the day talking about the message. Betin had fluently read the words on the paper, but didn't answer Dumphey's questions as to how he knew his letters—none of the peasants were allowed to learn their letters. He focused instead on the message. 'Twasn't clearly written out, but Dumphey deduced it to be an agreement of sorts, against the king. Four crowns had been included with the missive—enough to feed ten poor families in Abtshire for a week.

They had to take the message to the king. He and Betin hadn't yet decided by what means. The towns Fordyce, Metz, Kiralyn, and Haar stood between Abtshire and the king's castle. Lord Feroci had men spreading out as far as Metz. 'Twould make it difficult to travel there unseen. But if he could get to Kiralyn...

We'll have to overthrow Lord Kiralyn ... I will *obtain the throne.*

The words rang loud and clear in Dumphey's mind. Cold surged through his body. How had he not pieced together the words afore now? 'Twas Lord Feroci who had spoken those words—in anger. Dumphey sank to the ground. When had he heard them? He squeezed his eyes shut. Understanding erupted through him. This was why he was wanted in Abtshire. 'Twas why he was entrapped with the accusation of murder. They knew he had heard them.

He ground his fist into his leg. Why couldn't he have remembered the faint memory before? Why hadn't he taken more notice of these words? Suspected Lord Feroci before Betin shed light on Algor's findings? He had nigh forgotten the words that had drifted down to him. His faulty memory had endangered him and those around him.

But you remember now. His conscience prodded him to be grateful. Dumphey walked toward the vine curtain that blocked the cave's entrance from outside view. He wouldn't sleep tonight. He knew it wouldn't come, not with all of the thoughts peppering his mind. He stepped outside the cave.

God, what should I do? How long would Feroci wait before his plans were together and he formed an attack against one of the villages that lay between him and the king?

Silence. Was God not showing him the way because of the bribe he had taken? 'Twould serve Dumphey his due allotment. He studied the stars. It had been hours since the sun set in the horizon, giving way to a peaceful night, despite the worries and fears that roiled inside.

An evening dove called.

Again? Dumphey's heart thudded as he heard a second whistle—the one that warned them of upcoming danger.

He gave the return signal and walked forward as Patey neared.

"'Tis Noel."

The two words sank their teeth into Dumphey's soul, fear coursing through every vein. He grabbed Patey by the shoulders. "Where is he? What happened?" *Oh, God, protect my brother! Please, hear this prayer...*

Patey pushed away and glared. "This is the thanks I get for—"

"What has happened?" Dumphey put as much force behind his words as possible.

"He's not hurt." Patey broke eye contact. "Yet."

"Betin! Dickie, Arther!" Dumphey didn't care about keeping quiet lest soldiers were nearby. There were greater things at risk. Stefan was already returning to camp from his lookout, his eyes full of questions and caution.

"They have Lydda too."

Dumphey raised his brow. "Explain, lad."

Patey shifted as Betin and Dickie joined the group. "Barat put them in stocks this even—" He raised a hand when Dumphey lunged forward, but it wasn't enough to soften the rage that boiled under the surface. "I came here as soon as I could do so safely. Barat took a dozen knights and half the lord's foot soldiers away from Abtshire—the streets were dangerous until then."

If Dumphey were feeling compassionate—which he wasn't—he would take some pity on the lad's excursions. But Noel was in danger. "You promised to look after him!" He gripped his bow as he strode past Patey.

Patey didn't have an answer for that.

"Why did they take Noel?" Betin asked.

"And Lydda," Dumphey said, not allowing Patey the chance to lay the news more gently.

Fire flashed in Betin's eyes. "It has to be because of us. Lydda isn't the daring sort. I know she didn't break any law. The stocks are no place for her. One evening in the night air—"

"Aye," Dumphey agreed.

Dickie motioned toward the dimly lit sky. "If the lord follows the law of the land, they will not be in stocks by daylight."

Dumphey's head pounded. "Feroci doesn't follow the law." He ground his teeth. "He's trying to overthrow the law."

Stefan held Dumphey's quiver out to him.

Dumphey gripped it and gave a slight nod. "This is what we do. Encourage Feroci to follow the law." The lord may try to gain the throne by unjust means, but here in Abtshire Dumphey would do what he could to restrain his plans.

"And if not…" Dickie's eyes flashed in anticipation as he slid a finger across his throat.

"Nay," Dumphey and Betin said together.

"We will not slay anyone," Dumphey said, his resolve fading. He needed time to sort through things—not rush headlong into another encounter with the lord's men. But he hadn't time for that.

"Unless in defense of ourselves," Betin added. He grabbed his bow and rushed away from camp.

Dumphey ran after him. "Wait for us, Betin."

Betin stopped, but his green eyes flashed. "Feroci can come after me, I shall not complain. But if he touches my sister…"

Dumphey felt the same for Noel. He held out his bow. "We'll take the bows and surround them like we did last night. Just enough to confuse the soldiers and free Lydda and Noel." If necessary, they would use the daggers they had acquired.

Betin's jaw ticked and his Adam's apple bobbed. "I need answers."

So did Dumphey, but that had to wait. "When we near Abtshire, split up and surround the barracks from different points. We can't outnumber them, but we must outwit them." By the time they were back in town, 'twould be near daybreak.

Dumphey ran through the thick of the woods, eyes alert for guards, feet avoiding fallen branches and crevices. When the roofs of Abtshire came into view, he slowed. The moon was creeping toward the earth, casting a soft glow on the land. In the dim light, 'twas easy to slip through town. The nighttime guards were scarce—where had Barat taken them? To search for him? He took in deep breaths to calm the racing of his heart. He wasn't afraid of that. He couldn't be. Not when the lord had hands on Noel.

Encourage Feroci to follow the law. Aye, this Dumphey could do, and he was certain he could do it well. He clenched the bow tighter. 'Twas time to use his skills once again for good. He was fulfilling his purpose. He was doing what he should. But would it be enough against the lord's evil plans?

The sun was beginning to brighten the streets as Dumphey reached the stocks. Lord Feroci stood in front of Noel, his face dangerously close. Dumphey couldn't make out the words that were said, but he knew the threatening tone. His stomach churned as he watched. Two guards released Noel and pulled him to his feet.

"Now, over here." Feroci nodded to a wooden block.

The guards threw Noel on the ground beside it. He didn't make a sound. Dumphey's stomach lurched and he looked around. Patey stood nearest, still in the shadows, his bow ready. Betin was facing the stocks, and by his slight nod, Dumphey knew that he had made eye contact with Lydda. Stefan and Dickie were on the far side. They were ready and would act as soon as Dumphey gave the signal.

"Here is how I play," Feroci said. "I have ten questions for you. If you answer correctly, you get to keep your fingers. Every wrong answer, you lose a finger."

Dumphey didn't have to see Noel's face to know the stark fear that stimulated a harsh laugh from Feroci. He slipped an arrow from his quiver and placed it on his string, ready to draw.

"Where is Dumphey?"

"I know not."

"Ill-advised, my good lad!" The lord reached for his side and drew a dagger. He held it up in the faint sunlight. "I am truly a merciful man, Noel. You may have one more chance to answer the question." His voice turned hard as ice. "Where is he?"

Silence.

Feroci turned the dagger in his hand and raised an eyebrow. "I need an answer."

"Even if I knew, I would not tell you."

A thousand ants crept up Dumphey's skin. This was Noel—his shy, timid, fearful brother?

"Wrong answer!"

A soldier forced Noel's hand onto the block. Dumphey pulled back the arrow. Feroci bent closer. Dumphey released the arrow and drew another as the first embedded into the block.

Feroci froze.

"Here I am … *sir*." Dumphey raised his bow, ready to aim. "Where shall I aim next?" He made eye-contact with

Feroci. The man was enraged, which only bolstered Dumphey's courage. "Release my brother. If you have a quibble with me, then be a man and face me yourself. 'Tis cowardice to threaten a young lad."

Feroci straightened and turned toward Dumphey. "You call me a coward? You? When you were the one who ran and hid, leaving … *him* alone."

"What do you want, Feroci? I have taken nothing that is yours." Dumphey kept his arrow pointed toward the lord, ready for quick draw.

Feroci laughed. "Nothing that is mine? Son of a dead peasant wo—"

"My parents are dead, do not speak ill of them."

This only drew another laugh from the lord. "You are wrong, Dumphey." He took another step forward. "In so many things you are wrong."

Chills broke out inside Dumphey. There were many things he wanted to ask Feroci, but for now, he had one intention. "Release my brother."

Feroci came closer.

Dumphey shot an arrow at Feroci's feet then drew another. "I do not play games, Feroci. Release him."

"Or else what? You have no power. You have never had any power, and you never will."

Dumphey looked beyond Feroci to Betin. He gave a slow nod and Betin motioned to the others. They moved silently and quickly.

"Take another step closer, and my men will take action," Dumphey said. He pointed his chin as Dickie, Patey, and Stefan surrounded the guards.

Feroci turned and rolled his eyes. "Three untrained lads against armored guards. You're foolish, Dumphey."

"Yet I have managed to quite easily sneak into your well-guarded town of Abtshire. Twice. I have but one request of you: if you harm any family members of me or my lads, I will do more than simply threaten you."

"That is a threat, not a request," Feroci said. "And no one threatens the lord without paying for it."

Metal clashed and the group behind Feroci blurred. The lord turned and Dumphey sprang forward. Just a few feet behind Feroci, he called, "I have an arrow pointed at you. It will take me two seconds to draw and release. And I never miss my target—especially one this big. Command your guards to drop their weapons and step away."

Feroci turned his head and Dumphey released an arrow. It sliced the cape between Feroci's arm and body. "Now, Feroci."

Feroci growled and gave the command. Silence filled the morning air. Patey, Arther, and Dickie sprang forward and gathered the guards' swords that had clattered to the ground. Betin rushed to free Lydda and Stefan untied Noel.

"I have eyes here in Abtshire," Dumphey said. "But it is not Noel nor is it Lydda. Never again use a citizen for information or next time I shan't be so gracious."

The lord sniffed and turned his face toward Dumphey. His hard glare bore into Dumphey with a hatred he could feel.

"If you want me, you shall have to come out and get me yourself." Dumphey took a step back, his bow still at ready. The other lads dispersed, bringing Noel and Lydda with them.

They were almost out of sight when Feroci yelled, "Guards! After them!"

Chapter Sixteen

Noel ran beside Lydda, his heart beating a steady staccato in time with his feet. What had just happened back there? She was not with the lord after all?

They were following one lad—the others having dispersed. The lad clutched a bow much like the one that Dumphey had used. Where had they obtained weapons? Noel pushed the thought aside. They were in danger now. He knew it with every fiber of his being. Did this mean that he'd have to hide out with Dumphey and his lads?

The lad led them behind Commerce Row and slipped inside one of the shops. He pulled and pushed barrels, revealing a door on the floor. "In here, quick!"

Lydda grabbed a candle and flint from a nearby shelf and led the way down the shallow steps. Noel followed and ducked as he reached the last step. The room was only tall enough for the three to kneel inside. The dim light that filtered in through the doorway reached all four corners of the hiding place.

Muffled voices sounded outside, then the lad pulled the door and everything went dark. Noel stiffened as he heard Lydda and the lad shuffle around. The smell of earth wrapped around him. A spark flickered, then another. A small flame weakened then grew steady and illuminated the faces of Lydda and the lad.

"Lydda, you should save that."

"But I want to see you. You're really all right? I have been so worried for you. Where have you been? What happened the other night with the lads the lord captured?"

"Hush."

Noel watched the two as they stared at each other, unspoken communication going between them. This must be the brother Lydda had spoken of—Betin. The two looked near in age, the same smattering of freckles on their faces. However, where Betin's face was round and ruddy, Lydda's was slender and frail.

In the silence, Noel willed his heart to return to its normal rate. His fingers shook, and he clenched them together. "Where..." His voice came out squeaky when he tried to whisper. Betin and Lydda turned to him. "Where are we?"

"'Tis best if you know not," Betin said. "We'll wait until nightfall then make our escape."

"Escape where?" Noel didn't want to hear the answer, even if he guessed what it was.

Betin drew in a breath of air, and the candlelight flickered.

"You'll take me from Abtshire?" Lydda's voice was filled with hope.

Betin released a long sigh. "We may have no other choice. Why were you there—the stocks, Lydda?"

"I was worried for you," Lydda said.

Noel crept closer to the siblings. "'Tis my fault. I should have sent her away."

"Away from where?" Betin looked from Noel to Lydda.

"I … may have taken up work at the stables."

"Lydda!" Betin groaned and shook his head.

"'Tisn't a crime to speak to the stable boy, and 'twas my only way to get news of you," Lydda said.

"Everything is a crime in Abtshire with Feroci as lord! And your health. I canna lose you too, Lydda."

The cellar grew silent. Lydda set the candle on the ground and leaned back against the wall.

Noel gazed at the weak flicker of the light. Assuming Lydda was on Lord Feroci's side now seemed weak and foolish. He should have trusted her word more. "Lydda, I'm sorry…"

Lydda turned toward him. "For what, Noel?"

"I thought you were trying to glean information from me for Lord Feroci."

Shock filtered across Lydda's face and she blinked quickly. "But why—"

"You were a stranger, asking me many of the same questions as Barat."

"Nay! I just wanted to know of my brother."

"Aye." Noel's voice was hardly above a whisper. "I realize that now. 'Twas wrong of me. Forgive me?"

A small smile quivered on Lydda's face. "'Tis a trying time in Abtshire, aye. We know not who to trust—even those we've known for long. I forgive you."

Noel felt like sinking to the floor. 'Twas one thing made right this early morn. The room fell silent once more.

After a few moments, Lydda raised her open hands. "What do we do now?"

Betin gave a long sigh. The back of Noel's neck grew damp as he waited. He breathed in and out slowly, but his body still felt taut.

"We wait. And plan." He pulled out a pouch from under his tunic. He held it out to Noel.

"What is this?"

"Evidence."

Noel's heart dipped to his stomach. He didn't want to ask, but Betin was looking at him expectantly. "Evidence of what?"

"The lord's plot against the king."

"Nay, surely not." Noel knew that Lord Feroci was unjust, but to go against the king himself?

The barracks. The extra horses. The growing demand for soldiers. Noel had thought they were just to secure Abtshire, or the outcome of Feroci turning from sheriff to lord.

"'Twas intercepted. We read it, and the king must needs know of it."

"Betin, 'tis wonderful!" Lydda's face lit with hope and excitement.

"But…" Noel dropped his gaze to the pouch that held the key to Abtshire's freedom. "How can that be done?"

"Dumphey needs you to do it."

The words jolted Noel and his feelings warred against each other. Betin thought he could do such a task? At the same time that Noel himself thought of going to the king? Things that were so clear when he had the hope of freedom ahead were now foggy in the darkness of hiding from the lord's soldiers.

"Plans went awry because of your capture. I know not where Dumphey is, but the king needs to know of this immediately. You know Lady Lia and Lord Kiralyn. They can take the missive to the king. 'Tis the best plan I know of, but it must be done posthaste. The lord intends to put his plan into action within days."

Nothing in Noel wanted to receive Betin's words. But if he weren't to go alone… "If you come with me—"

"Two would be suspicious. Especially since Barat has taken the lord's men out of Abtshire."

"But two are better than one. What of Lydda?"

"Nay!" Betin was forceful even as Lydda looked eager. "Your health would slow you down. You know it, Lydda."

Betin held the pouch out to Noel. "If you just listen, I have a plan."

Noel eyed the pouch. In it was the key to change the future of Abtshire and to bring justice where tyranny prevailed. He closed his eyes and prayed. Was he brave enough to do it? Was he truly the one that God wanted to use?

Chapter Seventeen

Dumphey's head pounded as he raced through the forest. He hadn't heard anything in hours, but he wasn't going to stop until he knew he was safe. The Noch river ran beside him. He had purposefully led the soldiers opposite the direction of the cave. It might be nightfall before he got back, but 'twas a sacrifice he needed to make. He only prayed that the other lads were as wise and returned in safety.

As the terrain grew rocky, he slowed. It was now midday. The lord wouldn't give up his search quickly, but mayhap since Feroci had only half his men, they wouldn't be so spread out around Abtshire.

Pain tightened Dumphey's stomach. He clutched it and walked forward. When he returned to the cave, he would gladly eat something—whatever it was that Patey had brought in. He was too hungry to care where it had come from.

Feroci loathed him. He could clearly see it in his eyes. He had given little occasion for the lord to find fault with him—that one discussion Dumphey had overheard between him and Barat had been accidental. Surely that wasn't enough to put that hardened hatred in Feroci's eyes, was it? Or was it the freedom Dumphey had stolen for himself? Or the freedom of Cedric and his lads?

Even if it was, why did the lord take it out on Noel? Dumphey flung a branch out of his way then glanced around to be sure that no soldiers had been near to hear it. He held his breath. Regardless of which reason Feroci chose, 'twas because of Dumphey's actions that Noel was in danger. His choices had almost cost his brother his fingers—or more. Who was to say that Feroci would have stopped there? What did Feroci hope to gain by acquiring Dumphey's whereabouts? It wasn't as if Dumphey was taking action against Feroci's life—yet.

The wicked flee when no man pursueth: but the righteous are bold as a lion.

One of the Scriptures that Zuzene quoted slipped through Dumphey's mind. That must be it—the lord must think that Dumphey was pursuing him. He must assume that this was just the beginning.

Dumphey set his jaw. 'Twas correct. 'Twas just the beginning. But where was he going from here? If only he could go safely to Abtshire and speak with Zuzene. It had been ages since he'd seen her. He was certain that Noel would take care of her. But with both Noel and Dumphey in the lord's sights, who would see that Zuzene got her daily nourishment? Patey was good at sneaking in and out of places. Mayhap Dumphey could send him tonight. Yet...

He slowed his walk, a sudden yearning washing over him. In all of the excitement and changes, he hadn't realized how much he relied on his visits to Zuzene for her wisdom and guidance from the Scriptures. Another passage came to mind. *The steps of a good man are ordered by the Lord: and he delighteth in his way. Though he fall, he shall not be utterly cast down: for the Lord upholdeth him with his hand.*

Dumphey didn't know where any of the lads were, much less Noel and Lydda. He wanted to be bold like the lion Zuzene had told him of, but right now, all he felt was fear of the unknown.

He wanted his steps to be ordered by the Lord. But was he a good man? He ground his teeth. He accepted bribes, was tempted to bitterness and hatred. Aye, he was trying to bring order and justice back into Abtshire, but was he truly a good man—in the sight of God? Noel was always referring to God and following His ways... were they not desiring the same thing? Or had Dumphey been like the sons of Jacob, and had taken matters into his own hands?

He stopped. Doubts and guilt had tormented him for long enough. He would pause here—now—even in the midst of trouble and be sure his heart was pure and right before God. Dumphey didn't want to fall and be utterly cast down. He wanted the Lord to uphold him. He needed the Lord to direct his next steps.

If we confess our sins, He is faithful and just to forgive us our sins, and to cleanse us from all unrighteousness.

He needed that forgiveness. 'Twas too late to decide about whether or not taking the bribe was the right thing to do when God provided another way for him to escape the barracks. He could go for days feeling guilt about that decision, but 'twouldn't change anything. All he could do now was admit his wrong, confess his sin, and seek God for cleansing. *God, I can't put it into words, but Thou seest my heart and know my feelings. I have not trusted Thee like I ought to have and it has cost me. Forgive me.*

As he climbed the incline of the land, Dumphey prayed. Like Zuzene had taught him, he first found reasons to be thankful today—Patey had seen trouble brewing in time to save Noel and Lydda from whatever fate the lord had predestined, and Dumphey had gotten in and out of Abtshire unscathed. He only hoped that was true for the rest of his group.

He stopped and looked around. Branches swayed in the gentle breeze. Birds trilled their song as if everything was upright and just in the world. A squirrel circled its way around the trunk of a tree. Dumphey thought back to when Betin had first handed him the bow. Today, he would let the squirrel go free, even though he was certain he could take it down with ease.

He looked down at the bow in his hand. *'Tis a gift, God, and I haven't thanked Thee for it yet.* He walked into the brush. The squirrel scampered away and the birds paused their song. *Thou hast protected me thus far.* He stopped at those words. God was his refuge and strength—his protection. The same God would be the protection of Noel and the others—aye, He was the only One Who could protect those in Abtshire.

Dumphey had stooped to thinking that his strength alone would be the answer to Abtshire's problems. Instead of going immediately to the source of strength, he had tried to be the strength in and of himself.

The familiar trees surrounding a side entrance of the cave came into view. Dumphey took a deep breath and stepped forward. *God, let them be here. And if not, show me what it is Thou wouldst have me to do.*

A crunch broke the stillness beyond Dumphey. He froze. Stones skittered down the slope.

Dumphey took two steps back. The unmistakable metallic rustle of maille armor followed his movement. Dumphey looked behind him as he reached for his sling. With each step he took, he heard the step of a soldier. Dumphey prayed the soldier was moving as blindly as he was. In his brown clothes, he blended into the forest, but why could he not see the metal of the soldier's armor or a glimpse of red and yellow?

He was just three steps from the cave entrance, and he couldn't risk the intruder knowing the unguarded opening to their hideout. Dumphey stooped and grabbed three stones. He took a deep breath and waited for a moment. Nothing. He slipped the first stone into his sling, making a small loop. Silently, he flung the sling around and released a stone. It scampered into the brush several yards away. A second stone quickly followed the first, then the third.

The rustle of armor faded toward the stones. Dumphey ducked below the leaves that hid the cave entrance and slipped into the dark depths of the cave. He groped for a torch that Patey had placed at each entrance and left the shallow opening. No shouts had followed him, nothing that indicated he had been sighted. He lit the torch and took the tunnel to his left. There were tunnels of all sorts in this cave. He was grateful for the time that Patey and Betin had taken to give him a hasty tour through the depths. 'Twould be easy to get lost in here—which would come in handy if needed. But he didn't need to be lost now. He needed to find his lads and formulate a plan.

Waves of light kissed the stone walls around him before he turned the final corner to their camp.

"You're safe! Thank God!" Stefan stood from beside the fire.

Dumphey took in the relieved faces of Stefan, Patey, and Dickie. "Have you heard from Betin? Arther?" And Noel. They had to be safe.

"Nay. But ye know Betin," Patey said. "He shan't take risks." Instead of the usual scoff in his voice, he seemed subdued.

"We'll wait for him tonight. If he doesn't come, then we return tomorrow night," Dumphey said. Somehow, they'd make it past the soldiers that Feroci would have in the forest.

"'Twould be a plan," Dickie said, "except the lord is working to surround us."

"We don't know that for sure," Dumphey said. He willed it to not be so. He extinguished his torch and held it out to Patey. "Return this in case Betin comes to that entrance."

"Why? He knows these caves as well as me. He could find his way blindly." Patey took the torch and left still grumbling.

"We 'most got ourselves caught," Dickie said. The firelight played on the grin that grew on his face. "Patey was smarter than Feroci, though. Feroci knows we're here, but he doesn't know how."

Dumphey's heart sank at Dickie's words. His stones had probably only sealed the proof for the lord and his men.

Stefan sank onto a boulder, his broad shoulders squared as he looked up at Dumphey. "We peeked out not long ago. There are three guards within sight of this entrance and the two entrances east. I imagine soldiers are in between, where we could not see. I heard Feroci order the men then leave. He's coming back with more soldiers." He paused there and looked down at his hands.

He didn't have to say any more. Dumphey knew. They would be surrounded by morn.

Chapter Eighteen

oise scraped above them, then the door opened. Noel moved and winced. After a night in the stocks and hours cramped here, he wasn't sure his body would function.

"'Tis safe. Come out."

The male voice was unfamiliar, but Betin moved as if he trusted him. Noel waited for Betin to lead the way out of their safe haven then motioned for Lydda to go before him. He crawled up the earthen steps then forced his body to straighten out, groaning as every limb resisted movement.

"The lord has commissioned nearly all the rest of his soldiers to chase Dumphey in the forest. Only a handful is left here."

Noel straightened to look over Lydda's shoulder at the speaker. The lad was tall with a grim face and thatch of blond hair.

"So you are saying that we can get safely out of Abtshire," Betin said.

"Only if you're going the King's highway." The lad leaned against the wall and folded his arms. He looked comfortable here, no stranger. "Betin, do not attempt to rejoin the group. I would have been killed had I not turned back. Feroci has vowed to surround the mountain. He's sent a runner to fetch Barat and his army."

"But he doesn't know the entrances, does he?" For a moment, something like panic crept into Betin's voice. All of the time they were in hiding, Betin had kept a cool, calm attitude, reasoning with Lydda, assuring her of his safety, and making plans for their next move.

"You cannot think of going where the soldiers are," Lydda said. Betin shushed her, looking toward the main room of the shop.

"Arther and I will see Noel safely off, be sure he isn't followed. Then we must try to rejoin Dumphey and assist him." Betin turned and looked at Noel. "This fits into our plans perfectly."

Their plans. Fear seized Noel. He shrank back and shook his head. "I can't, Betin." He hadn't given his word.

"You must." Betin stepped around Lydda and laid a hand on Noel's shoulder. He gave it a squeeze which transferred comfort and strength at the same time. "Noel, 'tis your time to do something. There is nothing unlawful about our plans. We discussed this."

"But I never agreed." Noel couldn't speak above a whisper. Fear laced its fingers around his heart and squeezed any extra strength from him, leaving behind icy shivers. Slipping food to a hungry peasant was one thing. This? "I cannot... cannot..." He let his words fade into the crevices of the dim room. All three were looking at him. None of them understood. 'Twas written clearly on their faces.

Zuzene would understand. Zuzene would tell him what he should do. He took in a shuddering breath. "Is it safe for me to bring Zuzene a meal?"

The stranger nodded his head. "If we keep watch."

So, he knew Zuzene too. Must be one of Dumphey's men.

"Arther, Dumphey would never forgive us if anything happened."

The lad shrugged. "'Tis dark outside and I'll go with him."

Betin's brows furrowed. "Noel, don't waste your time."

Noel stiffened. "Time with Zuzene is never wasted. Please... let me see her before I make any decision?" Why did he have to bow to the orders of Betin? He was certain that Dumphey never did. But, he wasn't Dumphey. He could never be as strong and brave as his older brother.

"You must go alone," Betin said. "We cannot be seen together. We know not what spies are hiding in Abtshire. Fear not, though, Arther and I will keep a watch and be sure you're not followed."

Noel slipped a gaze to Arther then nodded. He didn't have a choice but to trust the lad. Surely if Betin knew him, and if Dumphey trusted Betin's judgment… Still, after all that had happened the past few days, Noel wasn't certain about Arther. If only he could speak to his brother—see him for more than a fleeting moment in the midst of a fight.

"Here," Lydda whispered. She removed a parcel from the shelf and held it out to Noel. "Take this to Zuzene. 'Twill be enough to keep her nourished until you return."

Until he returned. There was such finality in it.

Betin and Arther were talking in low voices to the side. They stopped when they noticed him looking at them.

"Stick to the sides of the cottages. Try not to speak with anyone. You'll be all right," Betin said. "We'll watch from a distance."

Noel nodded, but inside, his feelings revolted. No, he was not going to be all right. Not until Dumphey was home and the lord at peace with him. Which would likely be never.

Lydda gave Noel a gentle push. "Go along. I'll be praying for your safety."

Noel choked out a thanks, clutched the parcel in his hands, and walked out the door that Lydda held open for him. The shadows threatened him, as if eyes were veiled in the darkness.

What were the Scriptures that Zuzene said she quoted in darkness? And she lived in utter darkness. Noel shouldn't be scared of these shadows. But Zuzene's darkness never hid the threat of soldiers.

Noel noticed the pulsing of his fingers as they crushed the contents of the parcel. He breathed in and out and loosened his fingers. All ten fingers. God had sent Dumphey in time to save them. There was no doubt in his mind but that Lord Feroci would have taken them all. Noel shuddered. He would be helpless without his fingers.

The Lord my God will enlighten my darkness.

Aye, that was the verse. Noel mouthed the words, not daring to even whisper now that he was out of shelter.

The door of the shop opened and Lydda stuck her head out. She made a shooing motion with her hands. Noel stumbled a step then looked back. She was still waiting. He sucked in a lungful of air. She was praying for his safety. He could pray for his own safety. And where two or three agreed, God heard. Even if, like Paul and Silas in the Bible, Noel was cast into prison, God would have a purpose for it. Noel just hoped he didn't have to live through it and experience it. He wasn't brave like Paul.

He flattened himself against the wall of a shop. The plaster crumbled beneath the pressure of his body. He waited and looked around three times before going to the next shop. Then the next.

What if the lord decided to take out his vengeance on Zuzene? Surely as small as Abtshire was, Lord Feroci would know the connection that Dumphey had with Zuzene. Even if he hadn't been to the dungeon since he ran to the mountains. What was Dumphey doing in the mountains, anyway? And how had he found others to join him? How had they obtained weapons?

'Twould be nice to have a weapon now, since Noel was on his own and a target of the lord.

Some trust in chariots, and some in horses: but we will remember the name of the Lord our God.

A chariot and horse would be mighty fine to have. Noel would easily outrun Lord Feroci and his men. But the Name of the Lord was greater. Noel repeated the Psalm as he neared the dungeon. He waited for a guard to call out to him, but nothing happened. He crept forward, turning as he looked around. Surely the lord hadn't left Abtshire without any soldiers, had he? The momentary thrill that filled him with not having to watch his back was replaced with sick dread. If no one was here, that meant they were all after Dumphey and his handful of men. Mayhap they could outwit a few guards, but Noel was no fool. They were nothing against a well-trained army. Lord Feroci hadn't obtained the position over Abtshire and its province by being a coward.

Noel reached for the dungeon lock. There were tools in the stables that would easily loosen these chains. But should he? 'Twasn't his place. Or was it? As far as he knew, there was no written law against breaking into the dungeon merely to feed a prisoner who would starve without him.

Lord, show me Thy way. What am I to do here?

Calm peace washed over him as he headed toward the stables. With each step he took, he was more certain he was making the right choice. He slipped into the stables and past the rows of horses. He could feel the emptiness of it. Philaon must have gone home already, even though Noel hadn't been around to help all day. Guilt pushed at Noel's insides, but he ignored it. He'd make up with Philaon another time. For now, he had to get the tools to enter the dungeon. This was the sneakiest thing he had ever done. Yet was it not for a righteous cause? Zuzene mustn't starve, and he had to talk to her. He had to get some direction. Help. Wisdom. Anything.

Chapter Nineteen

"Who is it?" Zuzene's voice was feeble and slow.

"Noel." He stepped down onto the earthen floor. "I am sorry you've gone without food. I came as soon as I could."

"I've gone without before." Her matter-of-fact voice dipped to concern. "You're safe?"

"Aye." Noel knelt on the hard-packed ground and reached for Zuzene's hand. "For now. We are in great trouble, Zuzene, and I don't know what to do."

Zuzene took Noel's hands in her wrinkled, weak ones. "I knew the day was coming. I just hoped it would wait until you were older."

Noel slipped the parcel to Zuzene. "I was told there is enough in here for several days." He held to her hands as if they were the only steady thing in his life. In a way, she was. While the bustle of Abtshire had shifted and changed in the last year, Zuzene was here. She had always been here—suffering, but strong enough to endure. She had to endure. What would happen if she took ill while he was away?

"What will you do?" Zuzene asked.

"Do…?" Noel's words caught in his throat. He felt Zuzene move the parcel to the side. Her hand released his then rested on his cheek. 'Twas a cold hand, clammy from the dampness of the earth down here.

"You're a good lad, and I know that you weigh all of your choices with caution. I have no fear but that you will do exactly as God leads you to."

"I'm… I'm not sure of that." Noel hung his head as doubts pumped through his mind. He wasn't strong enough nor brave enough to do what seemed the next step to do. Why could God not ask this of someone else? Why him? Why not someone strong and fearless, like Dumphey?

"But you know what you need to do." The words were more of a statement than query.

Noel sucked in a lungful of the dank, earthy air. "Betin says I need to go to the king." Betin. Lydda. The lad, Arther. They all seemed in agreement. Yet they weren't the ones whose life was in danger—at least, not the type of danger that Noel found himself in. They could find a hiding place in Abtshire amongst the peasants. They weren't facing the wilds of the forest and threats of the lord's men.

With his voice low, Noel told Zuzene of the events of the past day, the reports of Dumphey's hiding place being surrounded. By the end, he had to force his words through his tight throat. This wasn't happening to them. Yet, it was. He couldn't deny it.

"I agree with your friends," Zuzene said. "In the multitude of counselors, there is safety. And you have many counselors who agree upon the same thing."

"But... why is this happening?" Noel drew his knees up to his chest and clamped his hands around them. He was still close enough to Zuzene where his toes touched the roughness of her garment. Were he a young lad, he would crawl into her lap, like he had when Mother had died, and let her comforting arms surround him. But he wasn't.

Silence surrounded them, and Noel focused on the pounding of his heart. It indicated moments quickly passing. Time with Zuzene that, if his efforts failed, would be his last here, with her.

"When evil men rule, 'tis cause for much chaos." Sadness deepened Zuzene's voice. "Tell me, Noel, what has been happening in Abtshire?"

Noel paused. Usually, Zuzene obtained news from Dumphey. From Noel, she merely wanted to know of his day and concerns. But then, rarely had he so great a connection to the goings-on of Abtshire as today.

He tried to think of all that had transpired since Dumphey's absence. The commissioned barracks was near completion—another week, mayhap, until the last brick was laid. The stables were filled with war horses and soldiers filled the streets of Abtshire—except tonight, when they were all out combing the forests for Dumphey. Noel prayed for his safety as he told Zuzene all he could.

When he finished speaking, she was quiet. "An uprising against the king, do you think?"

Noel clutched his hands even tighter. How did she deduce it this quickly when he had been blind to it until Betin's words?

"Has he sent his family off?"

"Nay. Lady Yzebel is still in Abtshire." Noel hadn't seen her, but from word passed among the peasants, he knew.

"And his children?"

His children? Noel wished he could see Zuzene's expression. "The lord hasn't any children."

"Ah." Zuzene didn't sound surprised. "Is there news of a babe on the way?"

"I know not." How would that affect the lord's choices? These things were too high for Noel to understand.

"You must go," Zuzene said. "While it is dark. Be safe, my child."

Noel nodded and stood. His heart pounded within him, and his knees buckled before he caught himself and stood upright. He could do this. He had to. There was no choice.

"Noel," Zuzene whispered. "Give me your hand."

He turned and reached until their hands once again clasped.

"Father God in heaven, hallowed be Thy Name. Thy kingdom come, Thy will be done." Zuzene squeezed Noel's hand tighter. "Tonight, Father, we thank Thee for Thy protection on the lads. I thank Thee for bringing Noel to me once more, and for providing again for my daily needs. I thank Thee for Thy mercy and grace. Now, Father, we ask for Thy will concerning Abtshire to be accomplished. Right the wrong, let truth prevail." Her voice grew stronger. "Dash the enemy's purposes against a stone, confound his plans, bring to silence his blade of injustice." She paused and her trembling thumb caressed Noel's hand. "Be with Noel as he goes to seek the king's help. Light his way, hide him from the eyes of the enemy, free him from fear, and give him Thy guidance with every step and every choice. Reassure him of Thy loving kindness and tender mercies. Thy will be done, Amen."

Noel kept his eyes closed, even though he was surrounded in darkness. Calm peace washed over him, replacing the terror he had felt moments ago. He wished to remember these words, to call them to mind as he left Abtshire behind.

"God go with you," Zuzene said, squeezing his hands again.

"Thank you." Noel held Zuzene's hand to his lips and pressed a kiss on the wrinkled fingers. He released them and felt his way back to the steps.

"Noel."

He stopped. "Aye?"

"When you bring the king, please..." her voice trembled, "find a way for me to speak with him."

The request threatened to drive away the peace that he was clinging to. This was real. He was leaving Abtshire. He would somehow, God willing, find a way to approach the king. Noel—nothing but a peasant. He steadied his breath and said, "Aye, most certainly." Of course, the king would find out the cause of Zuzene's prolonged imprisonment and bring justice. Why hadn't Noel thought beyond his own problems? He would pray for this to happen as he wandered into the unknown. 'Twould keep his mind away from his own dangers.

With a deep breath, he reached for the dungeon door. He paused and closed his eyes, relaxing in the peace he had found here. He would bring that peace with him, for God would not leave him alone out on the highway. He released his breath and opened the door. If he was never to return to Abtshire, he was ready. With God, he would do that which was directed him to do.

Chapter Twenty

*D*umphey paced the stone floor of the narrow alley between two cave rooms. Dickie and Stefan were relaxed, trying to get some sleep like he had recommended. Patey was scouting the other entrances. So far, no warning signal had been given, but that didn't stop Dumphey's body from tightening into a tense knot of nerves. His stomach clenched and he stopped to massage it. As soon as Patey was back, he would find something to fill it. He was hungry. That was all.

He sank onto a boulder and looked around him. They had erected a torch far enough from any opening so as not to reveal their entrance. The flicker didn't alleviate much of the darkness. Instead, it only made the darkness seem more oppressive.

He drew an arrow from his quiver. He had spent the last several hours searching the cave. Betin had a stack of wood that he had reserved for weapons in the future—curing, he called it. Better use the wood today than die, though. Dumphey had gone through the pieces many times, exploring the possibilities of an onager or trebuchet... but 'twas vain desires. The cave wasn't the proper place to use such a weapon, even if he could build something with their limited resources. The best he could come up with was a flaming onslaught—which was better used against a structure than from it. His hands were bound against options. They had a few dozen arrows, five daggers, and a few swords. Against over forty armed soldiers.

Father, they are so many, we are so few.

Shuffling notified him of Patey's return. Before he could ask, Patey volunteered, "They're camping out for the night. Two soldiers standing guard for every four asleep, from the looks of it."

Dumphey kept his face blank as he heard the report, but his stomach squeezed again. How long must they wait before taking action?

The torchlight glowed on Patey's face, reflecting the hard glint in his eyes that masked anything he was feeling. "Surely we can set some trap for them."

"But how long would that take?" Dumphey reached for his bow and passed it from hand to hand. The loosened string flopped, completely useless. At the moment, this was how Dumphey felt. Like a bowstring. Except he was a string taut and ready to release. Not idle, waiting for the master of the bow to ready him.

Am I a willing vessel in the Father's hand? The question seared into his mind, and he set the bow aside.

"How long can we last in here?"

Patey shrugged. "I didna exactly prepare for a siege."

Dumphey bit the tip of his tongue and tensed his jaw. It gave a slight pang from the messenger's kick the eve before. He listened for a moment, but all he could hear was the rattling breath of Dickie and a steady *drip* of water.

Patey slid down to the floor, his knees touching Dumphey's in the narrow space. "We've food enough to last six days. Eight days, if we use it carefully."

Though he wouldn't admit it, Dumphey was grateful for Patey's last raid through the lord's garner. 'Twasn't how he wanted to do things, but 'twas done.

Ask for help.

From Patey? Of all the scornful mockery in history. The very thought grated against Dumphey's being. The lad did what he wanted with no respect to Dumphey's wishes. Why would he stoop to ask his opinions now?

If only they had done more planning for defense of themselves instead of those in Abtshire. If only they had more time. But they didn't.

"If we could get word to Betin, he'd find the means to bring an attack from the other side while we defend in here."

Dumphey gave a mirthless laugh. "Too late. There are many things we could have done—should have done." Would he have known to do them, if he had spent even more time praying and less time scheming? 'Twas too late to know.

He studied Patey. His blond hair had grown a few inches, covering half his ears and sticking to his head in damp locks. His shoulders never stooped in defeat. Even now, Dumphey could read determination in Patey's whole frame. He would not give in. Not until his dying breath, if that's what it took.

Patey looked up and caught Dumphey's stare. His mouth twitched and he leaned forward. "We are like Gideon."

Dumphey raised his eyebrows.

"Ye know. The leader with few men against the army of thousands."

Gideon and the Midianites. A man from the Scriptures. Dumphey nodded his head slowly. "I'd not have expected to hear you likening us to a man of the Bible."

Patey sniffed and the left side of his lip turned up. "Mayhap I've never found myself in so desperate a place that I thought much of God and the Bible."

"But now?" Dumphey asked.

"Now... I am reminded of the truths that my mother shared before she passed on." He absently tapped the sword at his side.

Dumphey watched him for a moment, his heart pounding louder than when chased by the lord's guards. To run away from the enemy was simple compared to knowing the right words to say at the right moment, but Dumphey couldn't ignore the prompting to say *something*. Were he Noel, it would take him but a few seconds to lead into a conversation about Christ. But he wasn't Noel. 'Twas one thing to be bold in the face of danger; quite another to be bold in confronting a friend.

But they were facing possible death.

The thought loosened Dumphey's tongue. "What truths have you been thinking on the most?"

Patey looked at him, his brown eyes dark and brooding in the dim light. "Ye know... truths."

His answer was dismissive, but Dumphey wouldn't be able to live if something happened to Patey and this was where the conversation ended. He prayed for wisdom then asked, "Have you taken her words to heart?"

"Aye. I think." Still, he didn't sound sure.

"Can we talk about it?" Dumphey asked. If Patey said no, he wouldn't press. He'd have done his duty.

Patey shifted, his knees pushing into Dumphey then releasing as he settled further away. "I don't know as there is much to talk of." He looked down at his hands, which were now idle in front of him. He didn't say it, but Dumphey knew. He was scared.

"Death is real, Patey," Dumphey whispered. When Patey didn't flinch, he continued, "'Tis up to each of us to be prepared and ready, for when our time comes." There was fear in the unknown. As brave as Dumphey tried to be, the thought of how he would reach death sometimes paralyzed him. But he couldn't dwell on it. He had to think of all the beautiful promises that Zuzene had assured him of—how Jesus had gone to prepare a place for all who would believe on Him as the Son of God, how Jesus had paid the ultimate price and shed His precious blood so that all who believed in Him could be saved. Because of this, Dumphey was certain that when he took his last breath, he would be with Jesus in heaven. But what of Patey?

"Have you turned to Jesus Christ, relying in Him alone for the salvation of your soul?" Dumphey asked. The question was more blunt than he would have liked to have put it, but it was out there.

"I thought I did," Patey said. "But I don't think I was sincere. 'Twas so Mother would stop pestering me about it."

"And you haven't thought much of God since?"

Patey's chest expanded then collapsed. His fingers wove into each other and he lifted one shoulder in a half-shrug.

"Patey, 'tis important what you know now. If you have not lived for God and have cared nothing of what the Scriptures say, maybe 'tis because you said the words only—but didn't truly believe in your heart. Aye, 'tis with our mouths that we can tell others we believe, but 'tis with the heart that man believes unto righteousness. It requires repentance—changing our minds to agree with God. Is this what you believe?"

Another half-shrug.

"Only you can be certain of that." Dumphey wanted to shake Patey. He knew from the reckless way Patey acted that there was little fear of God in his heart. 'Twasn't his place to judge, though. He could only present the truth and let Patey decide for himself. How often had Zuzene done the very same for him?

Patey slid his feet toward him then stood, ducking his head so that he didn't hit it on the rock above him. "Well, if Gideon could find a way to outsmart the thousands, surely we can too."

Back to Gideon? "It doesn't work that way, Patey. Gideon followed God's commands. He didn't *want* to fight. God called him."

Patey grinned, though he didn't meet Dumphey's gaze. "About like ye and Betin. I still say we can use wit and wile."

"Mayhap…" Dumphey reached for his bow again. He couldn't force Patey to continue a conversation the lad didn't want. Still, something was unsettled in Dumphey's heart.

Ask for help.

He prayed in silence.

Help from Patey.

He lifted his eyes to meet Patey's. He tried to form words three times before they came out. "Have you any ideas?"

A grin stretched across Patey's face and he sat down again, this time leaning forward in eagerness. "I say we throw the lord off-track completely." He waited, as if to let his suggestion sink in.

"How so?" Dumphey asked.

"'Tis a far shot, but there is another entrance. If we leave now, we'll escape well before the lord even considers looking for it. They'll be waiting for us to make a peep and we'll be gone." Clearly, Patey was thrilled with this idea. 'Twas a game to him.

"You are certain they're not at that entrance?"

Patey shrugged. "Does Feroci even know of it? 'Tis two days' journey away from Abtshire—a day's journey to go through the tunnels. Feroci is in these areas. He's hoping to starve us out, ye know. 'Tis how he makes siege."

Dumphey had to agree. The plan sounded more promising than attempting to make weaponry without Betin's expertise. No warning signals clamored in his heart. If they set to work immediately, they would have everything gathered and ready to leave within the hour— hopefully, before the lord changed his mind and made a move.

Chapter Twenty-One

*H*orses raced past Noel. He crouched under low-hanging branches at the side of the highway. These were not the first horsemen he had seen tonight, and they probably wouldn't be the last. With every gasp of fear that threatened to sink its teeth into his heart, he repeated Zuzene's prayer, "Give him Thy guidance with every step and every choice." Every step.

The hoof beats faded. Noel touched the pouch that he had tied under his tunic, making sure it was still secure before he stepped back onto the highway. A light glow was beginning to thread its fingers on the horizon, hinting at the threat of full sun before long. Sometime within the night, Noel had passed through Fordyce. There were no other villages between him and Kiralyn Castle. He hadn't dared to speak to a soul that had passed him along the way. Rather, he had stayed well out of sight. With the threat of highwaymen or Feroci's soldiers, Noel wasn't going to take chances. And he had felt a peace about staying out of the way. 'Twas what was important, was it not? 'Twas how God had guided him in the past, and so far, it had kept him safe on his journey.

Now that light was beginning to illuminate the hard-packed road, he wasn't so sure about his next step. He kept to the side of the road. As far as he could see before and behind, there wasn't another soul out. He looked up, the sky's expanse widening before his eyes. Alone. For the first time in his life. There was no Dumphey to hide behind, no Zuzene to flee to for help. The fear that he had kept at bay when darkness surrounded him now crept into his heart as quickly as the sun's rays lightened the sky.

The road turned ahead of him, wrapping around a grove of trees. He slipped into the copse rather than stay in the open. A farmer's wagon rattled past, its wooden encasement barely visible through the foliage.

Just a farmer. No soldiers. He was safe. He would be. Had not Zuzene prayed for it? The trees thinned and he faced the road again. Three men were up ahead, their backs to him. They were in no hurry, laughing and talking as they passed under the shade of another grove of trees. Noel waited until they disappeared from sight before he stepped into the open. He jogged in time to his heart. His throat was parched from the night of activity without stopping. Just a few more miles, surely, and Kiralyn Castle would be up ahead.

Hooves clopped behind him. Noel stiffened and slowed, but refused to turn around. He was well out of the lord's province now. And Lord Feroci was busy hunting down Dumphey. He wouldn't think to send a scout after Noel, even if he was a runaway peasant. Besides, Betin had said they'd watch for followers before attempting to rejoin Dumphey.

But I'm not running away. Noel had to argue against his own mind. He wasn't running. He was seeking help. The two were vastly different.

The horseman kept his steady pace and passed Noel, flying colors that were not of Abtshire. Noel breathed in relief. He had given up counting how many times his heart had tripped over itself throughout this journey. Every time someone passed him, for certain. Why had he such little faith in God's ability to protect him, to answer prayer? 'Twas one thing to convince his mind of something. Another to live as if he believed it.

Father, forgive me. Protect me. Protect Dumphey. And Zuzene. And the others. The prayers tangled in his mind, preventing peace from taking over. He prayed again, the same words. His stride accelerated, then he broke into a full run. He had to flee these thoughts. This overwhelming fear that threatened what thread of peace he had left. Prayer was supposed to bring peace, not keep it at bay.

Now he entered the section of trees, and everything was shadowed again. Dark. Threatening. Foreboding.

Father God, I need Thy help! He clenched and unclenched his hands then wiped their sweat on his tunic. A patch of sunlight beamed ahead. A branch snapped on the path beside him. Noel turned his head to look, but didn't slow. A form moved behind the edge of trees.

His breath shortened. Chills snaked their fingers across his back then retracted, leaving behind threads of sweat. The trees spun around him. He just had to reach the clearing. Once he was there, he would be safe. His knees shook with each step. The clearing was just within reach. A shadow appeared beside him. Nay, 'twasn't a shadow. 'Twas a cloaked figure. A highwayman—in early daylight?

Noel's foot folded underneath him. He cried out as he thrashed to break his fall. His body slammed to the ground and the air rushed from his lungs. He lay there, gasping, but getting nothing. He hadn't any gold. No one knew of the pouch with the intercepted missive. He had nothing for the man to take from him except for his life.

Chapter Twenty-Two

Patey slid to a stop, and Dumphey's shoulder slammed into him. The light from the torch swung down then bobbed back up as Patey righted it.

"What are we stopping for?" Dickie hissed from the back of the line. It snaked around the eerie silence of the depths of the cave.

Dumphey turned his head only to be stopped. It had been several minutes since they had shifted to walking sideways, faces frontward. Or side-ward. Dumphey wasn't sure which direction it would be considered. He just knew that Patey had better be certain of this path or they'd be in trouble. Dismaying trouble.

"What do you see?" Dumphey asked. He had taken a big step, putting his trust in Patey. But since Betin wasn't here, he was the only lad who best knew the caves. Or so he'd said.

Patey mumbled a reply.

"Speak aloud. I cannot hear you turned away from me." Dumphey's body tingled, begging to be released from the hold of the tunnel.

Patey began moving—but not forward. He pushed at Dumphey with the hand behind him.

"We can't go back." Surely that was not what Patey meant.

Now, Patey's shoulder pressed into Dumphey's. The lad was smaller than Dumphey, but his meaning was clear.

No. This wasn't happening. It couldn't be happening. Dumphey braced himself, but Patey didn't relent.

'Twas about a hundred shuffle-steps back to where they could move their bodies. Just one hundred steps. Surely that time wouldn't be wasted to find out what Patey wanted.

Dumphey held up his left hand—the hand pinned behind him—and felt for Stefan. Just like Patey, he gave a shove. Stefan moved faster out of the way than he did, though, not seeming to question the digression.

The steps backward were faster than the steps they had taken forward, but that wasn't the cause of Dumphey's racing heart. The tunnel widened enough for Dumphey to turn his body, and he spun Patey to face him.

"What was that for?"

Patey didn't meet his gaze. "We canna go any further."

"Of all the scornful mockery in history!" Dickie sputtered.

Dumphey glared at Patey. "Impossible!"

"Ye felt how tight it was. The tunnel only got narrower."

"I thought you said it went through the mountain," Dumphey said. Perspiration inched its way down his neck and between his shoulder blades. Dark blotches swam before his eyes and he blinked them away, forcing himself to breathe slowly.

"It does."

"Where's the other tunnel?" There had to be another tunnel.

Patey turned his head away and responded, but his voice was muffled. Dumphey gripped his shoulder, his fingers digging into Patey's bones. He didn't care how hard he squeezed. He wouldn't relent until Patey looked his way again.

Patey shrugged his shoulder and turned again, this time, his eyes locking into Dumphey's. "I could make it as a child. 'Tis impossible now. Not even Noel would be able to fit through that crack. Stones obstruct it—they must have fallen."

Dust settled in Dumphey's throat, clogging it from saying anything.

"I've another plan, but we must get back. Now."

"All the way?" Dickie asked. "We've lost half a day already!"

"Aye." A look flashed across Patey's face, revealing the same vulnerability as earlier.

Dumphey took a stabilizing breath then coughed as rancid air filled his lungs. Between the bats and other creatures that found their abode in the cave, being back here only made Dumphey yearn for the fresh, woodsy air of the forest. He stepped back, leaving enough room for Patey to step in front of him. "You tried." The words were hard to say, but they needed to be said. "'Twas worth the try. What do you have in mind now?"

Patey stepped up, forming a tight circle with Dumphey, Stefan, and Dickie.

"We wait until nightfall and make our escape through the furthest west opening. Aye, Feroci has men watching it, but like we said earlier, he hopes to starve us out before he'd risk coming forward. He doesn't know we aren't well prepared. He'll treat this like a siege."

"Are you certain?" Dumphey asked. He wished he could muster up such assurance.

"I had ears when I visited the castle."

'Twas all Patey said, but it was sufficient. Patey had done more than steal rations in his time sneaking through Abtshire against Dumphey's will. Patey knew the lord's ways better than he did.

They retraced their steps in silence. The air seemed thicker than before, and Dumphey focused his attention on every step, following closely behind Patey's lead. His fingers were numb from their grip on the sack of food, and his quiver hung up on every rock they passed.

Patey stopped before they reached their destination and sank to the ground. "We've got to eat something. Keep up our strength."

"But not too much," Dumphey said. They hadn't food for even six days, like Patey thought.

"We'll be out of here in hours," Patey argued. "We need our strength." He took the bag from Dumphey and divided the portions of dried meat, stale bread, and bruised fruit. "Eat, drink, and be merry, my friends, for tomorrow, we may die."

Dickie laughed in mockery, but Dumphey studied Patey. The lad had lost his prideful swagger, and though his words were much the same, his tone was subdued. Dumphey could only pray that the words he had spoken earlier were taking root in Patey's heart.

They finished their meal in quick silence then were on the move again. If Feroci had grown impatient and searched for an entrance, he would have found the lads by now. The place they wished to be their refuge could very well be their death-sentence. Dumphey turned his attention to prayer. His thoughts roamed across things to be thankful for, from as early as he could remember anything. Those faint memories of Mother, still trying to coddle him like she coddled Noel, and how he'd refused since he was the man of the family. More vivid memories of Zuzene and the day that she was arrested and thrown in the dungeon without trial, how her face never flinched as she charged Dumphey to care for Noel and never to forget God. All of the visits to the dungeon—the horrible, dreary place as dark and hopeless as this cave. And Noel. Sweet, innocent, fearful Noel. 'Twas his childish tears that made Dumphey so brave in his early life. The tender heart that had helped Dumphey to become a better man than if he was left to his own rash decisions.

Dumphey swallowed, but the lump in his throat stayed. If today were his last day on earth, he would leave without a goodbye to Zuzene and Noel. Yet he was certain, beyond any shadow of doubt, that whatever pain he went through along the way, at the edge of death lay the glorious union of himself to his Savior, where there would be no tears nor death nor cruelty. 'Twould be well in the end.

Chapter Twenty-Three

The man grabbed Noel by his tunic and pulled him closer. A long beard and shaggy hair hid his facial features. All Noel could see was the open mouth with crooked, yellowed teeth, threatening him. "I know ye have something."

Noel's head snapped back as the man shook him. His teeth rammed into each other, and pain shot up his jaw. His limbs were like a limp leather harness. The man could shake him to death if he wanted.

"Are ye going to speak?"

Noel's chin trembled so much, he couldn't muster more than a moan.

"I gave ye a chance." The man raised his fist.

Blood pounded in Noel's ears, louder than horse hooves. Nay. They *were* horse hooves. Running toward him. The man's death-grip loosened as his curses filled the air, mingling with the shouts of another man. Noel sank to the ground, blinking against the blurriness in his eyes. Motion whirled around him. Feet pounded toward him. Footsteps faded away. Then nothing.

"Lad, are you hurt?"

Gentle hands touched his shoulder. Noel drew in a breath of air, then another.

"Steady, now. You are safe."

Noel eased himself up, helped by the same gentle hands. He brought his eyes to the man's.

"Ah, we've met before, have we not?" The man released Noel and stood.

A green and white doublet. The familiar smile. "You're..." It all pieced together. "Lord Kiralyn's man, aye?"

The man nodded. "Aye. Jolin. And you are one of Lady Ellia's friends. What brings you to this part of the country?"

Relief rushed through Noel. Why had he doubted and feared? God knew how to work all things out—much better than he could have planned himself. He placed his trembling fingers at his waist. The pouch was still secreted securely. Urgency pulsed through him. "I must find Lia. Immediately."

"I'm on my way there now." Jolin mounted then stretched a hand toward Noel and lifted him to the horse.

Noel clung to Jolin as the horse began. His heart was still pounding, but he calmed his voice to say, "I must thank you for saving my life."

"'Tis no matter."

A comfortable silence fell between them. Noel shut his eyes, soothing their dryness. The danger was far from over. Dumphey was still somewhere under the lord's grasp, but Noel forced his thoughts away from that. That was where he had been led astray earlier. He hadn't truly been praying—not like Zuzene had prayed. He had been focusing on the troubles that surrounded him and those he loved. *Father, Thou hast protected me when I doubted Thee.* Shame burned his cheeks. *Forgive me, Father. Help me to trust in Thee more.*

The ground beneath the horse changed, and Noel opened his eyes. They were passing through gates which led to a castle. Kiralyn Castle. Noel stared at it as they neared. Towers rose on various levels—far more than Lord Feroci's castle could boast. Rose-colored stone wrapped around the building, smoothing the connection from tower to wall, providing strength to the fortress.

Jolin stopped the horse and Noel slid to the ground.

"Follow me."

Unlike a servant, Jolin strode to the front entrance. As they walked up the steps to the gate, Noel slowed. It had been a long time. How would Lia see him, now that she was surrounded by such grandeur? Noel looked down at his clothes. They were caked with filth from the past few days' events. He didn't even have time to brush them before Jolin ushered him into the castle.

"Wait here." Jolin gave Noel a small smile that warmed him.

Noel nodded mutely and kept his eyes on the floor in front of him. 'Twas too late to rid his garment of the filth it had acquired now. 'Twasn't much worse than what Lia herself had worn but a year prior, but now she was a fine lady in the castle of her father.

Thoughts raced through Noel's mind. The events of the past few days jumbled together with the information that Betin had trusted him with. Information that could easily be discounted as the petty complaint of a peasant, if the king didn't credit the note they had found.

He couldn't move. Who was he, to be in such a place now? He was no Daniel to stand before even a lord. Nor was he eloquent to voice his thoughts as confidently as Betin had. He was a timid lad who would still be in Abtshire, had he not been pushed here.

A door opened and Noel's head jerked up. Jolin strode forward, his arms stretched out in a welcoming manner. "The family awaits to see you." His blue eyes twinkled as he added, "The young Ellia remembers you and your brother fondly. Had her health permitted, she would have traveled to Abtshire many times hence to visit you." He motioned for Noel to follow him. "She is delighted that you have finally made it out here to see her."

Though his words should have calmed Noel, he felt the familiar blood rushing to his head, causing his ears to pound and his vision to sway. Jolin led him through one doorway, then another. Voices became louder. Noel's bare feet were dry and crusty against the soft fabric that lined the walkway. He clasped his hands together, as if that would keep him from soiling the pleasantries around him.

Jolin glanced back with another smile as he stopped at a doorway.

This was it. Noel's mouth went dry and his knees grew feeble. He forced himself to take a step forward. Then another. What would he say? Why should Lord Kiralyn listen to him? Even if he sent for the king, would it be soon enough to save Dumphey? Would the king even care?

Chapter Twenty-Four

Now." Dumphey gave the signal quietly.

Dickie stepped out first. Dumphey could see his shadow move, but heard nothing. Good lad. Dumphey prayed he could make his escape without problem. Next, was Stefan. Then, Patey pushed Dumphey to walk ahead of him.

"Nay, I shall be last," Dumphey whispered in Patey's ear. 'Twas him Lord Feroci was after. If anyone must be left in the cave, let it be him.

He waited until he couldn't sense Patey's body nearby then walked to the entrance of the cave. It was shielded by a wall of brush that Stefan had erected days ago. 'Twould be shelter enough from the eyes of the guards. But the shelter wouldn't spread for long before Dumphey's back would be revealed to the guards. He could take no chances.

He grabbed hold of a tree that was rooted in the rock and pulled himself up the slick incline. The side of the mountain was the best road to safety, yet the hardest. He could hear the shuffle of the other lads in front of him. Compared to the sounds of night, 'twasn't much, but every motion sent a knife to Dumphey's stomach. He scooted up to the next hand-hold. His feet slid and a dozen pebbles scurried to the bottom like torrents of rain.

"Halt!"

Dumphey pulled himself up and gripped the next root. Then the next.

Armor clanked below him.

Dumphey reached one hand up, then his knee scooted up, then his other hand, then his foot. More rocks fled to the ground.

"You there! Stop!"

He ignored the threats and kept climbing.

A javelin clawed at the dirt beside him then tumbled down the steep slope. Close. Very close.

Father God, protect me. Protect us.

The ground flattened underneath him. He ran, his posture crouched. From the faint noise ahead of him, the others were making a speedy escape as well.

Another javelin skidded on the dirt below. The ground stopped against a sheet of rock. Dumphey looked up. There was no incline on this. Just flatness extending up to the heavens where stars winked at him. He turned and faced the soldiers below. In the darkness, he couldn't see them, but he could sense the gap between them lessening.

He shuffled on the path that led to a narrow ledge jutting out from the rock wall. The shadows of Stefan, Dickie, and Patey bobbed in front of him then blended with the brush. *Grant them speed, Father.*

His foot slipped and he groped for a hold above him. His fist slammed against rock as his other foot caught solid ground. He had to force himself to go slower. He slid his left foot forward, then his right. The yells behind grew louder. Another javelin glanced off the rock wall where Dumphey had just been. Another step, then another. His body pressed against the cold rock. His palms grew clammy. He moved forward. The ledge beneath him narrowed, giving way to black nothing below. He counted his steps. One, two, three, four, five...

A clash sounded in front of him as a javelin slammed against rock. Then another, closer. And another, this time behind him. Dumphey squeezed his eyes shut. Words flashed through his mind—something about enemies on the right hand and the left. The words failed him, but he used it as a prayer. He couldn't see where the missiles were coming from. *Father, misguide their aim.* He couldn't duck. He couldn't hide. He couldn't move.

When the javelins stopped coming, Dumphey opened his eyes. Everything was still dark around him. The faintest glimmer of light sparked—this time, well below him. He eased his way forward. Light flamed toward him and his heart tripped. A flying firebrand. He watched as it landed on the rock beneath him then fizzled into blackness. He took a dozen steps, one after another, but the damage was done. They knew where he was.

The javelins flew thicker, hitting below him, above him, and every few feet beside him. He kept going, praying with every step. His heart had stopped beating. His lungs weren't working. He was going to die. The thought pierced him just seconds before pain ripped through his leg and jerked him off the ledge, dragging him into the yawning openness of the abyss.

Chapter Twenty-Five

Noel wasn't given much of a chance to speak. As soon as he entered the room, Lia had peppered him with questions. But there were others in their presence—Lord and Lady Kiralyn and the young lady they introduced as their niece, Belle—so Noel kept his answers vague. Urgency quickened his pulse. He knew not what to say—or what to leave unspoken.

Noel focused his attention back to Lia—or, Lady Ellia, as she now was called, though Noel couldn't bring himself to change her name. She was paler than when he had last seen her, and didn't make any motion to move from her seat where a long, shimmering gown hid her deformed foot. But her whole demeanor was warm and welcoming. 'Twas hard to remember that this was the same lass who would limp into the stables every day to do heavy work—or, as heavy as Dumphey and Noel would allow her.

"Noel." Lia was studying him with a concerned look. "You aren't here simply to visit me, are you?"

Noel dropped his gaze to his hands folded on his lap.

"Please tell me. How are they really? Zuzene and Dumphey."

Noel's hands trembled and he clasped them together over his knees. He was sitting here, on a plush settee while Dumphey and his men were somewhere running from the threats of the lord. A lord that Noel was just now beginning to distrust more and more.

"'Tisn't good news you came to share..." Lia frowned and her brow furrowed. "Noel?"

Noel cleared his throat and looked from Lia to her mother to Belle, then finally to Lord Kiralyn and Jolin. All people that he could trust, yet his heart stuttered and his mind reeled to find the right words to say.

Lia straightened in her chair and leaned forward as if to rise, but her mother stopped her.

"'Tis Zuzene? Oh, I knew we should have tried harder to release her from the dungeon."

The look that Lord Kiralyn gave her was one of pain, understanding, and... helplessness? The faint glimmer of hope that Noel had harbored faded. Yet, had not God seen him safely here for a reason?

"'Tisn't Zuzene." At least, not yet. If the lord connected her to Dumphey and Noel, she may be next on his thoughts. Which was why he had to hurry. More than one life hung on this trip here. He closed his eyes and took a steadying breath. A firm hand rested on his shoulder and he looked up into Jolin's serious eyes. Rich blue eyes that encouraged strength and courage.

"From me, 'tis all hearsay." He dropped his eyes to the floor and took a deep breath. He briefly recounted the past few days of the lord's actions against his own village. Before he finished the tale of Dumphey's rescue, Lord Kiralyn began pacing and rubbing the back of his neck. When Noel paused for a breath, Lord Kiralyn moved as if to speak, but 'twas Belle's voice he heard first.

"This is done in Abtshire? And my father knows nothing of it?" She stood then took the seat beside Noel. "How is it that no one has tried to tell the king?"

"'Tis what I'm doing here." Noel's boldness faltered and he added, "If the king would even hear me."

"Oh, he shall hear of this." Belle stood once more and her cheery yellow skirts swooshed to catch up with her. There was such grace and confidence in her demeanor. "The king is my father."

Noel stumbled to his feet and stooped to bow. "Forgive me, I knew not—"

Princess Belle brushed aside his apology. "Uncle, what can we do?"

Lord Kiralyn hesitated and his words came out slowly. "We can tell the king of the mistreatment, but as of now, 'tis merely the peasant's word against the lord's. The king himself would have to send men to investigate. Which,

Noel here says the lord manipulates his people to give a good report."

Aye, 'twas what Betin had told him would likely be said. How Noel wished it was Betin standing here right now instead of him—a mere messenger-boy. He reached inside his tunic and withdrew the pouch. He forced his hands to steady as he held it, uncertain to whom he should give it.

"There is more than the lord's mistreatment, sir." He replayed the words that Betin had entrusted to him. "Dumphey and his men intercepted this note. 'Tis from Lord Alexandre. Something about…" He handed the note to Lord Kiralyn then glanced at Princess Belle, unsure of how he should proceed.

Lady Kiralyn and Lia bore mirrored expressions of confusion and interest. Jolin stepped from Noel's side to Lord Kiralyn and read over his shoulder—something that Lord Kiralyn didn't seem to mind, as he held the paper out for his man to see.

"The lad has a point," Jolin murmured.

Lord Kiralyn nodded, his thoughtful frown deepening. He handed the paper to Jolin and brought his gaze to Noel. "Come with me, please." He held up a hand to silence Princess Belle even before she spoke. "'Tis business with the king, not his daughter. I apologize, but 'tisn't your place yet, Belle." With a small smile to soften his words, Lord Kiralyn strode out of the room.

Noel jumped up and followed him down the hall and into a dark study. Jolin was but a pace behind and shut the door, enclosing them in the room.

"Have you noticed activity with more soldiers in Abtshire?" The congenial tone Lord Kiralyn had used earlier was replaced by one that was clipped and hurried.

More soldiers? The training had more than doubled since the sheriff gained his lordship. "Aye." Noel stood halfway between Lord Kiralyn, who was pacing by the window, and Jolin, who stood guard at the door. He shifted his weight from one foot to the other, praying that the information Betin had given him was enough to answer the questions Lord Kiralyn asked. Enough to move the lord to act on behalf of Dumphey. Mayhap, with Princess Belle here, that request would be granted with haste.

"Have you read this note, Noel?" Lord Kiralyn nodded toward Jolin.

"Nay."

Lord Kiralyn walked to the front of his desk and sat down on top it. "What type of activity have you noticed?"

A chill rushed through Noel's body and his throat tightened.

"You're not in Abtshire, lad." Lord Kiralyn's voice softened and the lines on his forehead lessened. "Until we get this matter straightened out, you will be under my protection."

The words were like a cup of cold water, refreshing and reviving Noel. All of the secrets that Lord Feroci and Barat attempted to keep in the stables could be safely spoken of here. Noel hadn't promised never to disclose them... he'd just been threatened to keep silent on the matter. "The lord has commissioned the building of a barracks. He is building up an army." He thought of the extra horses coming to the stables, and the strangers' horses he had cared for in the past few weeks. "He's had many visitors." His voice trailed off as he tried to think of anything else. Lord Kiralyn waited expectantly. Noel frowned and shook his head. Such little information was a failure, but 'twas all he had.

"You have shown yourself trustworthy in the past," Lord Kiralyn said. He folded his arms and looked Noel in the eye. "I desire to believe your word and to have the king investigate further." Hesitancy filtered through his features. "But if something is found lacking and your report was feigned, I cannot promise protection from the king or the lord any longer. Do you stand by your word?"

Noel shut his eyes as he thought on Lord Kiralyn's implications. Dumphey—aye, mayhap his life—was counting on him. Zuzene was praying for him. The lives of those in Abtshire were even hanging in the balance. For once, he had no doubts as he opened his eyes. "Aye, I am certain."

Chapter Twenty-Six

"Halt!"

There were those words again. The same words that had echoed in his mind, first loud, then soft, then deafening. He had stopped. He couldn't move. Could hardly breathe.

"Halt!"

The words mocked him. As if the soldiers couldn't see his near-lifeless form. Were they hovering over him now, or waiting for him to throw up his hands in surrender? He couldn't do that. Even if he wanted to, his arms were weighed down by something outside of himself.

"Halt!"

'Twasn't a command. Dumphey slowed his breathing and listened. There it was again. A bird. A gentle chirp. Nothing like the soldiers' harsh tones. Sunlight warmed his face. The thought of opening his eyes to its brightness made his head spin. The chirp sounded again. Where were the soldiers? The ones who were chasing him… but then, that was night. Was it night still? Was his mind deceiving him?

He groaned and forced his eyelids to move. A small sliver of light exploded and he squeezed his eyes shut again. Aye, 'twas day. Where were the soldiers? Why had they not taken him to the dungeon yet? Or, worse off, why hadn't they killed him? Were they tracking him, as one tracked an injured roe? Nay, they would have found him by now. Why hadn't they?

Dumphey pried his eyes open—fully open. Brown leaves shaded some of his face from the sun, but his eyes were fully exposed. He moved his hand, and leaves rustled under him. He tried his foot. Pain attacked him, and he gasped. He clenched his lower lip between his teeth. A metallic taste spread over his tongue. He swallowed then choked. He pressed his lips tight. He had to be quiet. If someone was waiting for him, he couldn't give himself away.

His eyes fell shut again. He opened them, this time looking beyond the leaves. Jagged edges of rock shelves created a frame around his vision. A solid gray barrier rose up to his right, leading to the pale blueness of the sky. Had he fallen from up there—and hit how many of those rocks? And he was still alive?

Pain throbbed in his head. What had happened to Patey? And Stefan and Dickie? Dumphey prayed they had made it to safety, that the soldiers hadn't gone after them once they knocked him down from his perch. And what of Noel? What had happened to him since the stocks? If only he could be certain that his brother was safe now.

Pebbles scattered from the ledge above him, bouncing as they hit the rock wall before sprinkling over him. Someone—or something—was up there. He moved his elbow to prop himself up. Darkness flashed bolder than the sunlight above him. He stopped and took three steadying breaths. Another handful of pebbles left the ledge above him. He eased his body up, biting his lip against the pain in his chest, his legs, his whole body. He couldn't escape. Not in this condition. He couldn't even make a shelter from the branches around him, shading him from scouts that were out to find him. He let himself back down and gripped his ribs as he took three more breaths. The expansion of his lungs drove tears to his eyes, but he blinked them away. He could pray. That was what he could do. Even if he was alone here, for days. He would pray. As long as he had breath, he would thank God and beseech him on behalf of his brother and the others.

The pebbles stopped falling from above him. The birds stopped their chirping. Even the breeze stopped blowing. Dumphey strained his ear to hear something— anything. Instead, dull silence surrounded him.

Then there was something. A distant commotion. He heard it now. Commands. Strong, screeching commands. Then the hushed, ominous sound of a multitude of swords being drawn. Whose swords? Or was that just the breeze again, brushing branch against branch? He sat up to see, sudden energy pulsing through his body. His hand pressed into a slab of wood and he looked down. His bow had landed beside him. Its string hung loose where it had snapped, but otherwise, the bow was unharmed. He reached to his side. The quiver was still there with arrows. Only two of them had been damaged by his fall. He reached to the bottom of the quiver and pulled out a piece of twine. Dark blotches spotted his vision and he stopped, breathing in with care. As soon as they cleared, he moved slowly. His fingers fumbled as he removed the broken twine then wrapped the loop of the new twine onto the tip of the bow. He stabilized himself with a lungful of air then stretched the twine until it reached the other end. With a quick movement, he forced the string onto the other tip and relaxed as it stayed put, energy draining from him like the rocks that were slipping from above.

He glanced up. Branches shadowed his vision, but there were men up there. Real men—not illusions. He braced himself against the pain throbbing from his leg and drew an arrow from his quiver.

"I know we got him, sir." A high-pitched, uncertain voice.

"You know nothing unless you have proof!" Lord Feroci. There was no mistaking his high-energy expulsion. "I didn't come up here for a foray with peasants. I ordered him dead. Do I see him dead?"

Dumphey's blood chilled. Between the branches, he could see the lord flanked by two soldiers. A shot to the lord's heart presented itself with no obstruction. Dumphey sat up straighter, moving slowly and silently. He notched his arrow and gritted his teeth as pain blasted through his body. His aim faltered as he raised the bow. He would have strength for one arrow and one arrow alone. Feroci moved and a branch stood between him and Dumphey. One step forward or backward and he'd be at the end of Dumphey's arrowhead.

"I will not have him steal my throne. Dumphey must die."

A vision of Zuzene in the dark dungeon flashed before Dumphey. Then Noel, his hand splayed out under a dagger threatening to remove his fingers. Lydda—an innocent lass in the stocks merely because her brother was hiding from the lord. Face after face of children, mothers, and fathers, ragged with hunger and exhaustion. Young lads training to fight at the lord's whims. Dumphey's thoughts were a fog then clear once more. Nay, 'twas Feroci who must die. 'Twould be the only solution to the tyranny and injustice he executed.

He clenched his teeth and willed the lord to move even as the strength drained from him. 'Twas his dying wish—

to free Abtshire from the clutches of Lord Feroci. He'd not live to see the result of his arrow. If Dumphey's injury didn't kill him, the soldiers beside Feroci would come down and do it. 'Twould be worth it, though. Freedom came at a price—someone always had to pay. And if Dumphey's life was what God demanded, he would do it.

The lord moved. Dumphey drew his arrow and looked down the shaft. The tip centered near Feroci's heart. One shot, and the lord would be wounded beyond recovery.

God, guide my arrow. The prayer passed through Dumphey's lips without volume. One shot was all he needed.

"I want you to find Barat and command him to search these woods until Dumphey is found."

The lord turned, exposing his chest. No armor protected it. Just a cape with the lord's red and yellow.

"What of the other lads?" one of the soldiers questioned.

"'Tis Dumphey I want. If the others come with him, all the better."

Is this what God would have you to do? The question pierced Dumphey's mind and his grip faltered. How he wished he could silence the childish worries of Noel. For so long, he had measured his actions for the lad's well-being. For the first time since he had left Abtshire, his course of action seemed so clear. Unknown to Feroci, the power was in Dumphey's hands.

The king's heart is in the hand of the Lord.

The bow and arrow lowered.

But Thou hast given me this opportunity. I didn't ask for it.

What would it mean to Abtshire, for Lord Feroci to be dead?

Thou shalt not kill.

What would it mean to Noel? Hope for a brighter future—with the memory of his brother murdering the lord haunting his life?

'Twasn't murder to exact judgment.

Yet what had David done, when King Saul was at his mercy?

Nothing.

Dumphey squeezed his eyes shut. Steps shuffled above him and faded. Judgment was of the Lord. Dumphey had to believe that and leave Lord Feroci's fate in God's trustworthy hands. He looked up where the lord and his men had been. Branches swayed, revealing that the target was gone. Dumphey laid his bow down and took in a shuddering breath. The lord would live today. Which meant Dumphey was in greater danger than ever before.

Chapter Twenty-Seven

Dumphey grabbed a branch and pulled himself forward, dragging his injured leg and scrambling for a foothold with his good one. The brush around him was a shield between him and the sky, but 'twouldn't be long before he reached the clearing ahead of him. His goal was the very same place that the lord had stood not long before. Because Feroci had been here, mayhap 'twould be longer before the lord's men searched this exact location. He couldn't wait until darkness fell. As much as his body yearned for rest, he had to press forward.

Voices created a backdrop of tension. They were even now searching for him. Dumphey secured his bow and quiver over his shoulder, sweat dripping down his forehead and into his eye. He blinked it away. *Father, I don't deserve Thy mercy, but I'm asking for it.* It felt wrong, asking for God to spare his life when but a short while before, he was willing to take the life of another. Yet 'twas hope in God's mercy that propelled him to move forward.

He reached up for the ledge above him. If he could pull himself onto the rock surface and lie flat, he'd make his way to the next incline hidden with bushes. He leapt up and his fingers clamped onto the rock.

"Not now."

Dumphey froze. Hands rested on top of his fingers.

"They're still in sight."

Panic eased as his mind registered Patey's voice.

"I can't hang on for long," Dumphey whispered. Everything hurt now, from his fingertips to his feet.

Patey shifted above Dumphey and moved to grip Dumphey's wrists.

"They're moving. Just give them one moment more."

"You should have fled," Dumphey said, gritting the words out as a flash of pain pulsed through his body.

Patey didn't answer. When Dumphey's fingers loosened their grip, he felt Patey's grip tighten around his wrist.

"Come up now. Ready?"

Dumphey used his good leg to propel him upward. Patey pulled until Dumphey's torso was above the ledge. He bit back a groan as Patey grabbed his leg to bring him all the way up.

"We can't stop yet. There's a pathway that will take us away from the soldiers. Ye must move fast." Patey's eyes darted to the leg that Dumphey had attempted to bandage then back to Dumphey's face. "'Tis a climb of about two hundred steps, then there's a flat rock we can scoot across. We're ahead of them now. We must keep it that way."

He turned and led the way. Patey was like a mountain goat on the rocks; Dumphey, slow and clumsy as his throbbing leg kept him back. Once again, Patey had been a God-send—the most unlikely answer to prayer. An odd sense of camaraderie was forming betwixt the two of them, replacing the times of disagreements they'd had.

A shout echoed up the mountain and Dumphey crouched down, clinging to the trunk of a crooked tree. Patey slid beside him and craned his neck. Distant clashes of metal against metal backed the noise of men's voices.

"What is happening?" Dumphey asked.

Patey shook his head as he stood to his feet. "I canna see." He looked down at Dumphey. "We should continue."

This time, Patey didn't keep back for Dumphey, but scrambled to the next table of rock. When Dumphey collapsed onto the flat ledge, a smile stretched across Patey's face. "I told you God could use us like Gideon."

Confusion clouded Dumphey's mind. Nay, 'twas a heavy fog as dull as the midnight sky. The questions forming in his mind dissipated to nothing, and Patey's smile switched to alarm just a moment before he disappeared into black fog.

Chapter Twenty-Eight

*I*ncessant shaking jarred Dumphey. Water rushed over his face and he sputtered. He was drowning. He clawed his hands forward and opened his eyes. Instead of water enveloping him, there was Patey. And Stefan. Dumphey wiped his hand over his face and coughed. The pain wasn't as bad as earlier. He looked down at his leg. Someone had wrapped it in crude bandaging.

"Finally," Patey grumbled. Yet his eyes held a gleam that couldn't be dampened. "Ye must see this!"

Stefan helped Dumphey to a sitting position as Patey leapt ahead of them. Dickie was already at the edge, looking down. Dumphey stumbled to his feet and staggered the first few steps then steadied himself against the dull ache in his leg and pushed forward until he was with the others.

Swords clashed and shields reflected the fiery glow of the late-evening sun.

"I don't understand," Dumphey said as a battlefield spread before him. He rubbed his head, wishing that he could just as easily rub sense into it.

"'Tis the king's own men!" Dickie did a half-jig as he said the words. "Their colors—ah! What glorious blue and gray! What say you? That we come down from above and give him a hand?"

Dumphey looked from Dickie to Patey then Stefan. "We don't kill." The words caught in his throat as awareness of his actions from earlier flooded over him.

"But we can drive them down into the king's arms, aye?" 'Twas more of a challenge than a question from Patey.

Dumphey felt his side for his quiver, only to claw at fabric.

Stefan gave him a hint of a grin and retraced his steps to where Dumphey was lying earlier. He brought the bow and quiver to Dumphey and handed it to him in silence. In that moment, Dumphey sent up a quick prayer for direction. Nothing. No peace, no clarity, no impression for the next steps to take. Just a small thought trickling through his mind.

Pray with them.

He looked at the boyish faces surrounding him. Their gazes were expectant and eager—just as they had been the night they had lay wait in Abtshire, ready to requite Feroci for attempting another unjust hanging. They were nothing against the lord's men, but if they could keep them from escaping up the mountains, like Patey suggested...

Still, peace refused to come. Dumphey tried to push away the incessant prodding to pray—aloud—with his men. There wasn't much time for a decision. "Mayhap..." The lads' attention focused on him and uncomfortable silence rested on them for one heartbeat. Dumphey cleared his throat and continued, "Mayhap we should seek God's counsel. Together."

"Aye," Stefan was the first to agree, and bowed his head, expectantly.

Dumphey didn't wait to see what the others did, but folded his hands over the smooth wood of his bow and squeezed his eyes shut. "Father God, I thank Thee for sparing my life today." *I thank Thee for keeping me from killing Feroci.* He didn't add the words aloud, but he was grateful. "I thank Thee for sparing the lives of my lads. I thank Thee for bringing the king's men here. Give us wisdom what steps we are to take, whether—"

A sword dully leaving its sheath interrupted Dumphey and he spun around, pulling an arrow from his quiver. Two men in the lord's red and yellow stood, swords drawn.

"Methinks here's our answer," Patey said.

Dumphey felt his men circle around him, creating a wall of bows and arrows.

"We've the king's men on our side," Dickie shouted. His voice squeaked with boyish enthusiasm.

"I see no one here to help you." The front soldier took a step forward, his sword ready for a thrust. "The king's men are well below us."

No killing. Dumphey slid his arrow onto the string and aimed. The fingers that wrapped around the sword were bare. A small target, but a target nonetheless. He drew then released.

Blood splattered onto the sword's hilt as the soldier reeled backward. With a shout, Patey and Dickie lunged, releasing arrows as they ran toward the soldiers. Dumphey and Stefan followed.

The soldiers scrambled down the slope until they reached a place with boulders. The rocks formed a shield around them, forcing Dumphey and his lads to stop.

"Be ready," Dumphey whispered. He didn't know what the soldiers were planning, but they wouldn't be caught unawares. 'Twould be a slow pace to force the men down to where the king was, but if it took till the evening, Dumphey was willing to try. First, he had to get the soldiers back in his sight.

He slung his bow over his shoulder and gripped a trunk suspended from between two boulders. He pulled up and steadied his hands on the rock. He groped for a small ledge. As soon as his fingers found it, he inched his way up until he was on top of the boulders. Another pile of rocks blocked his path, hiding in the fog his brain created.

He blinked and steadied himself before limping up the rocks, blocking out the pain coursing through his entire body. There was a ledge just beyond. If he could reach it, it would place him directly above the men.

A quartet of yells blended together, sending chills up Dumphey's back. They were rushing his lads. He leapt over to the ledge. Pain shot through his leg and his sight dimmed.

Help me, Father. For their sake.

He caught himself on the boulder with his arms and upper body. As soon as his fingers found something solid, he pulled himself fully up. Daggers of pain knifed his leg as he used it to force himself upward. He landed on the top and stopped for a moment, catching his breath. A shadow fell over him. He glanced up. Two soldiers cloaked in Lord Feroci's colors stood on the rise above him, their focus on the scuffle of Dumphey's lads below.

Heart racing, Dumphey forced himself to move slowly. He pulled himself into a crouching position, careful to not brush against the pebbles that dusted the top of the boulder. He reached for his bow and an arrow. One of the men was a mere foot-soldier. He hadn't the full armor of a knight, but skin was exposed on his legs and arms. Plenty of places for Dumphey to target without taking his life.

The soldier rubbed his hand along the spear he held. From their placement, they could probably see the lads on the plateau clearly.

The soldier's body tensed and he raised the spear. Dumphey grabbed a second and third arrow, placing them between his other fingers, ready for quick draws. The breeze around him froze into stillness. All he heard was the rushing of blood in his ears as he waited. As soon as the soldier drew the spear back, Dumphey released his first arrow. It sank into the soldier's forearm. The spear clattered to the ground and rolled down the mountain as the soldier cried out. The second soldier, who wore full body armor, turned to Dumphey.

Dumphey notched the next arrow and planted it in the unarmored part of the soldier's leg. He scooted as far back as he dared while he readied his third arrow. The fully-armored soldier drew his sword. Though his face was shadowed by helmet, Dumphey could see the grim lines in his face—was it determination, or fear? He didn't look much older than Dumphey himself. If he dared remove his helmet, Dumphey would likely recognize him from his time in the barracks.

"Leave my men be, and I'll spare your lives," Dumphey commanded. "I haven't a quarrel with you." Surely they knew that with the king nearby, their army was sorely outnumbered.

Neither soldier moved.

"Tell them to retreat." Dumphey kept his voice low and even. "I do not miss my aim." He kept his gaze on the armored soldier.

The soldier turned to look at his companion who was visibly striving to hide the pain from Dumphey's first arrow. "Fall back!" The command held a tone of hesitancy.

Dumphey nodded toward the soldiers' weapons. "Drop them. Tell your men to do the same."

The soldier's knuckles on the sword whitened then he tossed the sword to the rocks below. One moment of hesitation, then the soldiers below him followed.

"Now," Dumphey said. "Make your way down there. I'm immediately behind you with an arrow at your back. Hurry."

He gritted against the pain in his leg as he slid down the mountain behind the soldiers. The other soldiers were surrounded by his men, their weapons in Patey's and Dickie's hands.

"Over there." Dumphey limped as he followed behind the soldiers. He loosed the sling from his waist and tossed it to Patey. "Tie their hands so we can lead them down."

Patey gleefully took charge of the men, ordering them around. He secured the last one when a long, mournful horn sounded from the valley, rippling its way up the mountains. Dumphey looked from the soldiers to his men. Something had changed in the battle between the armies of the king and Lord Feroci.

Chapter Twenty-Nine

*T*was over. The king's men were disarming Lord Feroci's soldiers. Abtshire was safe once more. Noel turned his eyes upward and gave a prayer of thanks to God. Betin and Arther stood beside him, having joined up with the king's men as soon as they entered Abtshire.

Lord Kiralyn had tried to persuade him to stay behind as the men went out to battle, but Noel couldn't. Not when his brother's life was in danger. He couldn't see from here, though. He left Betin and Arther behind and pushed his way through the king's soldiers until he stood beside Jolin.

"Have you seen him?" Noel's body tensed as he asked the question. Soldiers marched in front of him, rounding up Lord Feroci's men in red and yellow. Seeing them now didn't strike fear in Noel's heart like before. But then, they weren't in command here. They were in defeat.

"All we've seen are Feroci's men."

Had Dumphey been successful in hiding, then? Noel's blood chilled as two of the king's men neared, Lord Feroci between. He stood, head held high, jaw jutted out, and a determined glint in his eyes.

The lord spat on the ground when he was near Noel. "You think your brother won, aye?" His voice was coarse and loud. "Or, should I say the lad who masquerades as your brother?"

Masquerades? *Don't heed his words,* Noel tried to assure himself. His breath caught in his lungs and he couldn't think of a response.

Jolin laid a hand on Noel's shoulders. The lord was just angry and spouting out whatever he could to get Noel riled. He wouldn't succeed though. Noel took a deep breath and straightened his shoulders.

"Aye, do not let him deceive you. You're not his real flesh and blood. Ask Zuzene—she knows."

Noel's eyes widened before he could stop himself.

The lord chuckled. "I am speaking the truth. Though, if Dumphey even knew the truth of it, he couldn't tell you now. Maybe his blood will speak for him—from his grave."

Noel lunged forward. He didn't dare touch the lord. But he stood close enough so the lord could hear his quiet, tremulous voice. "Where is Dumphey?"

"He fell." The lord nodded his head toward the mountain. "Ask my men. We all saw him. I wish 'twas my javelin. The filthy wretch—"

"Silence." Jolin was beside Noel again, towering over the lord. "Methinks you have spoken enough."

Lord Feroci didn't reply. He only gave Noel a long, hard look that made him feel as small as a field mouse.

Noel turned to Jolin and whispered, "We must find him."

Jolin pushed him away from the lord and together they walked to the place where the mountain began its steep ascent. Noel craned his neck as he took in the massive structure before him.

"If he truly fell…" He blinked back the tears that blocked his voice as he scanned the sheer rock face. If Dumphey had fallen, could he survive without his body being broken in pieces? Noel had seen men come in from the fields, injured. There was never much hope for them. Even less for the soldiers who returned with wounds crudely bandaged.

"Noel, look." Jolin pointed to a place hidden by undergrowth.

At first, all Noel could see was the movement of bushes. Then, a lad appeared—Patey. Noel dashed forward and plowed into him.

"Slow there!" Patey pushed him back. "I may be excited the king's men are here, but—"

"Where is Dumphey? Please tell me you know."

"Noel."

The clamor of the soldiers surrounding them faded as Dumphey limped toward him, held to his feet by two of his men.

A loud curse snaked from behind, jarring the moment. "You are dead!"

Dumphey placed an arm around Noel's shoulders, leaning on him heavily. His chest heaved as he calmly looked toward the lord.

"Nay," Patey said. He marched up to Lord Feroci and stood, toe-to-toe with him. "I'd be counting your blessings, not cursing were I ye. Ye could be the one dying this instant. He spared your life." Patey pointed back to Dumphey.

Noel looked up at his brother, awe filling him.

"Aye, I saw it myself," Patey said. "Dumphey was lying where ye left him to die. He had his bow drawn, aimed at your heart." He leaned forward and jabbed a finger at Lord Feroci's chest. "I wish he would have released that arrow, but he didn't." He took a step back. He was no longer talking to Feroci. He turned and faced Dumphey. "I'd give my hand to know why."

Dumphey lowered his gaze to the ground and Noel saw his Adam's apple bob. His brother was having a hard time with the words. Noel wrapped his arm around Dumphey's middle and squeezed. Dumphey glanced down with a smile.

"I thought of you, Noel," he said. "And all of those Bible stories you grasped better than I. David had a man's life in his hands more than once, and he refused to do the job that belonged to God." Dumphey looked toward the lord. "Your life is in God's hands. Not my own."

Admiration surged through Noel. Dumphey was a man of action. A man who did things more than think them through. Yet, he hadn't let his actions lead him astray. He opened his mouth to praise Dumphey when the king rode up. The soldiers and subjects bowed as the king and Lord Kiralyn stopped before them.

"Are all your men here, Dumphey?" Lord Kiralyn asked.

Dumphey looked around at the three lads beside him. "These are all who were with me."

The king dismounted and stood before Dumphey. "I shall see to it that you are rewarded for your bravery."

"Nay!" Lord Feroci roared and fought against the men holding him. "He deserves no reward for fighting against the law you placed in the land, Your Majesty." His dark eyes gored into Noel before turning to Dumphey. "You, of all people, should know the degradation of a child turning against their parent. Will you reward this lad for leading a rebellion... against his own father?"

Dumphey's arm tightened around Noel then his head slumped forward and he slid out of Noel's grasp to the ground.

Chapter Thirty

*D*umphey limped through the dark halls. Sconces hung on the walls where lanterns should give a glow, but they hadn't been lit. And he didn't command them to be. Nay, today was a day when things were changing around Abtshire, and he needed the quiet darkness to think.

It had been one week since the king's army had surrounded Abtshire and set things to right. Feroci and Barat were being tried for treason, likely to be executed as the king's law commanded. Even now, the king's armies were following the trail of those who had signed an agreement with Feroci to overthrow the king's rule. Things would be well in the kingdom once more.

Yet all was not quite right in Abtshire.

Dumphey paused as another hallway opened to him—this one well-lit. He laid his head back against the smooth stone wall. In the room just two doors down, Noel was sitting at Zuzene's bedside, entertaining her with his little stories and tales of the day. Dumphey hadn't seen Zuzene since the day the king released her from the dungeon. Guilt tore at him, mixing with dread and turmoil. She had been pale—so pale—when he finally laid eyes on her in daylight. Years in the darkness of the dungeon had weakened her and left her blind. Yet 'twasn't that which held Dumphey back.

She was his grandmother, aye. But she was Feroci's mother. He, Feroci's son.

He understood her honor in keeping the truth from him, but it didn't ease the pain that tore his gut every time he thought of it. Feroci had left his wife for the riches and promises of Lady Yzebel—for the position of sheriff.

A throat cleared behind him and Dumphey turned. Betin gave him a slight nod then glanced toward Zuzene's door.

"Feroci..." Dumphey couldn't bring himself to acknowledge him as anything but that. "He cast his own mother into the dungeon for speaking God's truth. He let his wife die in poverty while he... he embraced the comfort of riches. Of *sin*."

Betin placed a hand on Dumphey's shoulder.

"All those years when Zuzene encouraged me to do what is just and true—those very acts kept her down in the dungeon." Even after Dumphey's mother had died,

Feroci's bitterness and anger had kept Zuzene hidden away.

"She knew the cost and deemed obedience to God worthwhile."

Dumphey folded his arms in front of him. "Aye." He could admire that of her. 'Twasn't her place to tell him that Feroci was his father. What if he had known, all those years ago? Would that have changed the way he looked at life? Would he have rejected Zuzene's teachings and embraced the pleasantries of a sheriff's son? A lord's son?

He met Betin's compassionate gaze. "Feroci knew I would never follow in his footsteps. He was satisfied to kill me—his *son*." And hope that his new heir—the upcoming child of Yzebel—would be one that he could mold to be just like him.

"Dumphey." 'Twas a mix of rebuke and compassion.

Dumphey straightened his shoulders and gave Betin a half smile. "I shall forgive him—I must forgive him."

Betin nodded.

"'Tis a lot, aye?"

This time, Betin gave him a full grin. "From outcast to the lord of the province? Aye. Never you worry, though. I shall keep you straight."

"I shall need it."

Jolin would be here on the morrow to counsel Dumphey for a few months. But for now, 'twas just Dumphey in the lord's castle—his castle.

217

He looked once more to the door then at Betin. "If you'll excuse me."

He took the stone stairs opposite that led up into gaping darkness. His hands guided him along the wall as he took each step. His injured leg was stiff and slow, but he pushed himself forward until he bumped into a door. He fumbled for the handle then opened it. Sunlight exploded, lighting the dark interior and inviting Dumphey onto the top of one of the castle's towers.

As he stepped from the darkness to light, a sense of freedom followed him. This was Abtshire—leaving the darkness to the hope of brighter times. He walked to where a window was carved from the stone, overlooking the streets of Abtshire.

Father God, Thou hast brought me here. The weight of his words slammed into him and he stopped. For the first time in all that had transpired, he felt tears come to the surface. He blinked them back and faced the sky. 'Twas a bold blue today without any clouds marring its blank slate. *I thank Thee for freeing Abtshire of Lord Feroci.* His throat tightened and the thanksgiving he felt froze into the confusion of knowledge he had been trying to sort out.

Pain wove through Dumphey's heart as he thought of Zuzene. She was freed from the dungeon at last, like he had prayed for years. Yet how long would she live in the comforts that Dumphey was able to provide before she took her last breath? She was so weak, so frail.

And Noel—his cousin, the son of his mother's sister. Zuzene had said that Noel was nary a year when his parents passed and he joined their family. He'd always be his brother, regardless of their birth. Compassionate, helpful Noel. While Dumphey was always quick to act physically, Noel was quicker to extend mercy and love. Dumphey prayed that would never change in Noel. Though Zuzene's words shocked Noel as much as Dumphey, 'twas Noel, the shy, timid one, who had reassured Zuzene—a woman who was no blood relation to him—of his love, appreciation, and support. Aye, there were still a few things that Dumphey could learn from his younger brother.

I want to be a man who follows after Thy heart, Father. In so many ways, he needed to follow God's Word in order to be an upright leader. 'Twould take time and patience to learn all he needed to be. He had much to sort out as the new lord of Abtshire. His thoughts turned to prayer once more. *I am undeserving to be in this position. Like Solomon of old, I need Thy wisdom and direction. Apart from Thy grace, I would be Feroci.* A shudder ran through him, but he knew 'twas true. The only hope for Abtshire was what could be done through the strength of Jesus Christ.

He had fought for weeks in the forests of Abtshire and had hidden in the depths of the cave. He had lived when he should have died. Zuzene had always assured him that God had a special plan for him still. And mayhap the plan was for him to see light shine once more in Abtshire.

Epilogue

Dumphey continued as the lord of Abtshire, ruling his people with wisdom, justice, and equity. A year after he was fully established as lord, he took Lady Ellia—or Lia, as he preferred to call her—as his bride. She continued to struggle with her health, but otherwise lived a comfortable life. They raised a family of two children—a little lass named Zuzene, and a lad named Raoul.

Zuzene spent the rest of her days in the warm care that Dumphey provided. She didn't live to see her great-grandchildren, but her legacy lived on in the hearts of Dumphey, Lia, and those who knew her.

Noel decided to become a man of the Word and left Abtshire so he could share God's Word with others struggling to trust Him. He traveled throughout various villages in the king's domain and never married.

Dumphey's lads and Lydda stayed in Abtshire as ardent supporters of their new lord. Betin became Dumphey's right-hand man. Stefan married Lydda. Patey and Dickie settled down as they matured, and Dumphey placed them over his army. Arther chose to work in the stables as Philaon's new stable-hand.

Lord and Lady Kiralyn visited Abtshire as often as time permitted, leaving Jolin to oversee the duties at Kiralyn Castle.

The king continued to make progress in becoming invested in his domain and judging according to the principles of God's Word. He found a worthy and suitable husband for his daughter in Prince Durant. Prince Durant and Princess Belle had four children: Little Durant, Elayne, Bryant, and Lecia.

There were always the poor in Abtshire, but Dumphey saw to it that they never went without food and shelter. Injustice and cruelty faded from the streets of Abtshire and merry-making finally lightened the end of each day's labor.

Discussion Questions

1) Which character do you most identify with? Bold, brash Dumphey or timid, faithful Noel? How were they both able to live for God with their different personalities?

2) Was it Biblically right or wrong for Dumphey to have accepted the bribe? How would God have provided a way out for him, had he not accepted the bribe? Can you think of any Biblical examples where an individual leaned on their own understanding instead of following God?

3) Throughout the book, both Noel and Dumphey grew in their prayer life. How is your prayer life? Do you remember to stop and thank God—even when you're in the middle of trouble? How can you grow in your own prayer life?

4) Dumphey had to make the choice to stand against his friends stealing from Lord Feroci. Zuzene had to take a stand against her own son and ended up in the dungeon. Why is it important to stand on God's Word rather than go with the flow? Have you ever had to make a difficult stand

when others were doing wrong? What will help you to take a stand next time?

5) Both Noel and Dumphey were impacted by Zuzene's knowledge of Scripture and faith in God. Do you have a godly friend you can go to who will point you to Scripture? How can you make decisions today that will help *you* to become a faithful Christian like Zuzene was so that you can point others to God's Word?

6) Betin said, "Every man has a choice. He can choose blindness concerning the evil that surrounds him, or he can choose to make a difference." Have you considered the choice you have?

7) Have you ever been like Patey, where you've come face to face with the reality of death and your relationship with God? Patey was given more time to evaluate his answers, but no one is guaranteed tomorrow. Are you truly trusting in God for salvation?

8) Noel realized that he wasn't really praying, but only thinking about his worry. Have you ever done that? What are ways you can take your thoughts off your worry and genuinely "cast your cares upon the Lord?" (1 Peter 5:9)

9) Zuzene had spent years in the dungeon, yet her faith never wavered. How do you think she was able to keep that solid faith?

10) Dumphey received a staggering blow in the end of the book with the truth about his father. Though he struggled, he knew what he had to do. What was that choice he had to make? Did he push that choice off to another day, or make the choice right away?

Scripture Passages

Chapter 7
For whosoever shall keep the whole law, and yet offend in one point, he is guilty of all. (James 2:10)
Recompense to no man evil for evil. Provide things honest in the sight of all men. (Romans 12:17)

Chapter 8
Dearly beloved, avenge not yourselves, but rather give place unto wrath: for it is written, Vengeance is mine; I will repay, saith the Lord. (Romans 12:19)

Chapter 9
Brethren, I count not myself to have apprehended: but this one thing I do, forgetting those things which are behind, and reaching forth unto those things which are before, I press toward the mark for the prize of the high calling of God in Christ Jesus. (Philippians 3:13-14)

Chapter 17
The wicked flee when no man pursueth: but the righteous are bold as a lion. (Proverbs 28:1)

The steps of a good man are ordered by the LORD: and he delighteth in his way. Though he fall, he shall not be utterly cast down: for the LORD upholdeth him with his hand. (Psalms 37:23-24)

If we confess our sins, he is faithful and just to forgive us our sins, and to cleanse us from all unrighteousness. (1 John 1:9)

Chapter 18
For thou wilt light my candle: the LORD my God will enlighten my darkness. (Psalms 18:28)

Some trust in chariots, and some in horses: but we will remember the name of the LORD our God. (Psalms 20:7)

Chapter 20
For with the heart man believeth unto righteousness; and with the mouth confession is made unto salvation. (Romans 10:10)

Chapter 24
A thousand shall fall at thy side, and ten thousand at thy right hand; but it shall not come nigh thee. (Psalms 91:7)

Chapter 26
The king's heart is in the hand of the LORD, as the rivers of water: he turneth it whithersoever he will. (Proverbs 21:1)

Thou shalt not kill. (Exodus 20:13)

Historical Note

While the *Tales of Faith* series has a fantasy flavor—in that the exact era, country, lands, castles, and characters are completely from my imagination—I have made it a point to include some true historical elements. Being that it is not exclusively historical fiction, I have taken some liberties with dialogue and terminology that may sound too modern. But when it comes to village life, soldiers, weaponry, clothing, and food, I have tried to use enough historical accuracy to make it believable.

Bow-making and archery was a specific subject I kept as historically accurate as possible. Small things like using fur to silence the bowstring, holding more than one arrow in the hand to shoot faster, loosening the bowstring when not in use, and not drawing the bow and holding it for a long time before shooting, are all fruits of research.

Author's Note

When the pages closed on "The Secret Slipper," I knew there had to be at least one more story from these people. Robin Hood has pretty much always been a favorite classic tale of mine. As soon as I realized Dumphey could fill the role of a Robin Hood type of guy, I knew exactly how the series would end. It was, at times, brutal to write because I felt I couldn't truly do a retelling of Robin Hood justice. There were so many plot bunnies that begged me to follow them, but I had to narrow it down to keep it within the realm of a novella, thanks to the shortness of the previous two books.

The conclusion of a series is always bittersweet. I have loved journeying through the lives of Belle, Lord Kiralyn, Lia, Dumphey, and Noel, and hope you have too. My readers' enthusiasm for "Befriending the Beast" and "The Secret Slipper" has been a fine motivator to get book three finished and out to the public.

Every time I complete a project, I am in awe of the amazing support group with which God has blessed me. No author writes alone, and this author for sure does not. I am going to forget someone, I realize, because this project has been over a year in the making, and I have failed to keep arduous notes as people have stepped out and helped me. So if you're not listed, know that you're among one of those whose help I appreciate deeply, but my faulty memory fails me.

Christopher - you happily lent me your Bowyer's Bible series and answered many of my bow-making questions.

Rachel - you helped me brainstorm and develop the group we all love: Dumphey's "Merry Men." Thanks for helping me figure out a diversity between Dumphey, Patey, Dickie, Betin, Stefan, and Arther.

Emily - you have read this manuscript more than anyone else (besides me). Your input and Robin Hood enthusiasm has helped me so much!

Anita and Faith - you were both accountability partners when I needed someone to be sure I kept on track with actually working. This book wouldn't be here without that kind of help!

My alpha readers - you read a pretty rough batch of manuscript and your comments gave me the direction I needed to polish this up and make it actually presentable.

My beta readers - your enthusiasm and critiques have helped me to be a better writer, once again.

My readers - if you're reading this, then *you*. An author wouldn't be of much use if there was no one to read her work. It warms my heart every time I know that someone has read and enjoyed my stories, and it humbles me when God has used my words to bless and encourage a reader. Thank you for reading—and for sharing your thoughts about my work with others.

My family - you support my passion for writing, whether it is by bragging on me (*rolls eyes*) or by reading my work and giving me constructive criticism.

Mom - once again, you've pulled through as my line editor. Thank you!

My heavenly Father - every book You have me write, You weave in a lesson for me to learn and apply. Thank You that You're not done working in my life.

As always, I hope that you come away from this story with more than an appreciation for a good tale. I pray that the struggles Dumphey and Noel went through spiritually help you in your Christian walk, and that the lessons they learned will be ones you can embrace as you grow in the Lord.

While I'm sad to leave this kingdom behind in my writing, I have learned so much through this journey as a writer and am thankful to the Lord for helping me not only generate ideas, but also see them to fruition. To Him alone be glory!

Amanda Tero

Connect with Amanda

Email: amandaterobooks@gmail.com
Website: www.amandatero.com
Facebook: www.facebook.com/amandateroauthor
Instagram: amandateroauthor
Pinterest: amandaruthtero
Blog: www.withajoyfulnoise.blogspot.com
Goodreads: AmandaTero

MORE BY AMANDA TERO

Short Stories
Coffee Cake Days
Finding Christmas Joy
Hartly Manor
Letter of Love
(short story sequel to "Journey to Love")
Letters from a Scatter-Brained Sister
Maggie's Hope Chest
Noelle's Gift
Peace, Be Still
Quest for Leviathan

Novellas
Journey to Love

Tales of Faith Series
Befriending the Beast
The Secret Slipper
Protecting the Poor

Non-Fiction
Me? Teach Piano?

Have you met the Master Author?

The "author and finisher of our faith," the "author of salvation?"

Well, why do we need to know the Master Author?

There is no man, woman, boy, or girl who is without sin. Romans 3:23 says, "For **all** have sinned, and come short of the glory of God;"

Have you lied, cheated, stolen, taken God's Name in vain, coveted, or lusted? All of these are sins according to God's Holy law (see Exodus 20). Even if we neglect in just one area of God's law, we are found sinners. "For whosoever shall keep the whole law, and yet offend in one point, he is guilty of all." (James 2:10) The payment for sin is death ("For the wages of sin is death;" Romans 6:23a)

God does not desire to leave us in this hopeless, destitute state. He did what we could not do and paid the debt for us. He sent His Son, Jesus Christ, to come, be born of a virgin, live a sinless, perfect life, die a cruel death, and rise again, victorious over sin, death, and hell! Romans 6:23 continues to say, "but the gift of God is eternal life through Jesus Christ our Lord." Jesus Christ is the only way to have eternal life, to be forgiven ("Jesus saith unto him, I am the way, the truth, and the life: no man cometh unto the Father, but by me." John 14:6). God promised us that, "If we confess our sins, He is faithful and just to forgive us our sins, and to cleanse us from all unrighteousness." (1 John 1:9)

Salvation comes by putting your faith and trust in Jesus Christ for salvation and eternity ("Believe on the Lord Jesus Christ, and thou shalt be saved, " Acts 16:31) and repenting from our sins ("Repent ye therefore, and be converted, that your sins may be blotted out," Acts 3:19).

So, have you met the Author?